Letters to Helen

Kayt Roth

LETTERS TO HELEN

©2013 Kayt Roth

A Wandering Minds Publishing book.
North Vancouver, BC
www.kaytroth.com

ISBN Number: 978-0-9919-180-1-0, 978-0-9919180-0-3

First Edition: April 2013

Published and Printed in Canada

For Jantine

The best cheerleader and friend a girl could ask for.

Chapter 1

Music rattled the windows in a lone country house, loud enough for wisps to drift across to neighboring farms. The beat reverberated off every surface as it traveled to the speakers that ran through the house, keeping the cook company as she prepared the evening meal. She sang along, dancing in place as she busily spread butter over top of the assembled shepherd's pie. In perfect time to the music, Mattie licked the spoon clean, tossed it in the sink, slammed the lid down onto the roaster and twisted the dial to set the oven, all while continuing to dance her way through her work.

Once dinner was in the oven she danced into the dining room, where her grandmother's china had been housed in the glass and oak cabinet. Her mother had objected when she took it along to the new home she rented with her fiancé, but Mattie had felt it was the perfect addition to the large, rather impersonal house. She continued to sing as she set the table, laying out a place setting at each end. Standing back to admire her handiwork, she noticed that something was missing.

The music paused as the CD carousel changed discs, leaving her to hum to herself as she climbed the stairs to the second floor. It kicked in again as she entered the master bedroom, a smoother and more melodic tune than before. "Candles…candles…" she muttered, digging through the dresser drawers as she searched for a paper bag that had been rolled around the object inside it. "Ah hah!" Unrolling the bag with a flourish, she started to dance again as she removed two tapered candles, then pirouetted to drop the remainder back into the underwear drawer before bumping it closed with her hip.

The grandfather clock downstairs chimed seven o'clock – he would be home in about half an hour. She moved on to the walk-in closet, trying to decide what she should wear for dinner that night. The concept of dressing for dinner was new to her – but then again, the concept of dinner that wasn't eaten in the car was also new to her. Mattie wanted desperately to be more of an adult, insisting that she and John sit down to home cooked meals as often as they could.

Clothes started to fly in all directions as she rifled through outfit after outfit, frowning into the mirror each time she stood back to look at herself. She had gained about twenty pounds since graduating from high school three years before, and though John's income ensured that she could afford clothes that fit her, nothing she bought ever seemed to look right. Finally, she decided on a button-down, knee-length blue dress – one that usually managed to get his attention.

The clock sang again, half an hour passing by in a flash. "Oh shit!" She hurriedly kicked all the discarded clothing back into a corner of the closet and raced back downstairs, getting halfway down before she came back to retrieve the candles that had been forgotten on the bed.

The candles were set out on the table as the timer for dinner clicked off. A turn of a knob lowered the music's volume, and the press of a button changed the mood from exuberant to romantic. Before Mattie could leave the living room, she caught a glimpse of herself in the large picture window. Purposely standing in profile, she sucked her stomach in as she ran her hand down the front of her body. The results were not encouraging, everything falling back into place with a grieved huff. She struck a sex kitten pose, a much more flattering angle that gave her generous curves and soothed her anxiety. *Too bad I can't always stand like this.*

"Ah well," she mumbled, looking out past her reflection as she waited to see headlights as he returned home. He wasn't there yet, so she returned to the kitchen – but not before bumping up the volume on the stereo just a little.

John Frost stood at the high portion of the receptionist's desk as he made notes in his patients' charts from that day. The clinic was empty, everyone else having left just a few minutes before. Being the last one out at night was not unusual for him – he had become a workaholic very soon after starting his own practice.

He looked up when someone knocked on the door. Maria Hawthorne stood there in the pouring rain, hair stuck to her forehead and knuckles white as she knocked on the glass. He frowned as he rounded the desk, quickly unlocked the door and pulled her inside. "What are you doing here?"

She was stiff, moving only at his insistence so he could shut the door behind her. "I wanted to catch you before you left," she said quietly.

He led her back into his office, where he showed her to the visitor's chair on the other side of his desk. It seemed like she was in shock, numb to everything around her. "What's going on?" he asked her as he took the seat next to her. "You okay?"

Her head shook slowly, but it took her a long time to find her voice. "John…" Her nerve quickly dissolved. So instead she reached into her purse and handed him a picture, curled at the ends from when it was shoved inside.

John looked down to see that it was an image from an ultrasound – with a fetus that was about eight weeks old, and Maria's name in plain type at the top. He looked at her, then stared down at the photo again. "What's this?" he finally asked her.

She smiled slightly. "It's your baby."

"What?" John's mouth fell open. "Are you sure?"

Maria flashed with anger. "Of course I'm sure!"

He slouched back into his chair, his stare alternating between her and the photo. "It can't be mine."

Tears started rolling down her face – she had known he wouldn't be thrilled, but she had hoped that he would have taken the news better than this. "You're the only one I love," she reminded him. He got up, feeling the need to put some distance between them. "Why would I lie to you about a baby?" she challenged when he didn't answer her.

"What am I going to do?" he worried to himself as he began pacing the length of his small office. Then he suddenly told her, "You have to get rid of it."

Maria couldn't believe what she had just heard. "I what…?"

His pacing sped up, but he glared at her when he told her again, "You have to get rid of it."

"I'm not getting rid of our baby!"

"You have to!" he shouted at her. His hands rifled through his hair as his panic grew. "Christ, Mattie's going to kill me."

Maria sensed that she was about to be told something she didn't want to hear. "You said you were going to leave her!"

"I never said I was going to leave her for you." His expression cooled, but anger was foremost in his words. "I won't be trapped into a marriage with you, Maria."

His statement stabbed at her. "I didn't get pregnant on purpose, John. It was an accident."

"I don't care," he retorted. "And unless you want to lose your job, you'll get rid of it."

Maria stood up to her full height and dared him, "You can't get me fired from the hospital."

"Just watch me," he threatened. "I'll make sure you never work as a nurse again."

She glared at him, disturbed by what had just happened. Turning to leave, she spat at him, "You son of a bitch!" Then she fled, barely noticing the rain that continued to pour down and re-soak her as she fought to get the key in the car door.

"Kim, I'm back!"

The front door of the house flew open with enough force that the knob made a dent in the drywall behind it. Graham Martin struggled past the screen door with several heavy bags of groceries in each hand, cursing loudly when the bottom edge of the door caught his heel. He stumbled into the kitchen and heaved the bags up onto the counter. "I think I got the paper towels you wanted, but you'd better take a look."

When he turned around he saw his girlfriend at the bottom of the stairs, overnight bag in hand, trying to sneak past him without being detected. She managed to get about three steps toward the door before he called after her, "Kim?"

She let out a squawk of surprise, obviously caught as she spun around. "Oh hi," she gasped, her hand covering her pounding heart. "I didn't hear you come in."

He eyed her for a moment, then said, "I've been loud enough to wake the dead."

Her lips pursed as her eyes darted around the room, landing everywhere except him. "Yeah...well..."

"Well what?" he questioned, taking a tentative step toward her. He could tell that she hadn't been as shocked as she tried to portray – and when her keys jingled in her hand, it drew his attention to the bag. "So...where are you off to?" he asked, not coming off nearly as lighthearted as he wanted to.

"Um..." She looked down at the bag in her hand, suddenly realizing that he wasn't stupid. But she couldn't quite bring herself to tell him the truth. "I'm going to Seattle," she said brightly, pasting an unconvincing smile on her face.

"Really?" He took another step toward her. "When will you be back?"

"I – I'm not sure." There was silence, and when his eyes finally met hers, she knew she couldn't lie to him anymore. "I'm moving out," she said flatly. "Darren and I have gotten a place downtown."

He had known something was up, but this wasn't the answer he was expecting. "You what?"

Kim glanced down at her shoes, unable to look at him anymore. "Graham, I didn't want you to find out like this."

He glared at her. "Looks like you didn't want me to find out at all."

Any pretense she had of being nice flew out the window. "Look, what do you want from me?"

"Well an explanation would be a good start! You said it was over with Darren!"

"I…" She started to say something, then thought better of it. Instead she just opted for, "I'm sorry," and then bolted for the door.

"Kim!" He raced after her, but wasn't able to catch her before she slammed the door shut on her car and locked it. "Wait a minute!" he yelled through the glass. "Kim, wait!"

Tears were already streaming down her cheeks as she started the engine and slammed into reverse. "Leave me alone!" she shouted at him as the car started to move. He was so engrossed in trying to get her attention that she nearly hit him with the front end when it swung to turn into the street. Then with a screech of the tires she disappeared down the street.

Graham stood there for a little while, trying to process what had just happened. Eventually he realized that a few of the neighbors who had been out on their lawns had witnessed everything and were now staring at him, a mixture of sympathy and embarrassment for him radiating from each.

Not knowing what else to do, he went back inside. The grocery bags sat on the counter, mocking him from across the entry. His daze took him into the kitchen, where the bags just seemed to remind him that they had been the distraction Kim needed to escape. But escape from what he didn't know.

The groceries clattered to the floor when he hurled them across the room, vegetables and fruit shattering on the tile floor when they hit. His roar of agony vibrated through the windows, but still left him hollow when it was over. What made it worse is that she left with no good reason, save for her stunted explanation of moving in with the man she had cheated on him with.

Chapter 2

Black thoughts swirled and converged within Mattie's mind as she waited for the other chair to be filled, the only outward sign of her agitation being the continuous drumming of her fingers. Self-imposed darkness surrounded her, broken by the small circles of unstable light thrown from the candles. Since she started them two hours before they had been slowly disintegrating, rivulets of molten wax dripping down onto the tablecloth below. Beyond the lights were the barest outlines of her sophisticated dinner setting and the very cold remains of what was supposed to be a romantic dinner for two.

The clock struck the quarter hour, filling her ears with its melody and her heart with even more anger. He was beyond late. Fifteen minutes could be forgiven. Even an hour. Now he had attained the rank of either completely forgot or didn't want to bother, depending on how he decided to handle it when he finally got home.

She extinguished the candles when the clock marked the bottom of the third hour, emptied the wine bottle and took her glass out onto the patio. A car was driving past in the distance, the sound of its motor carried on the cool breeze that now made her shiver. The temperature had dropped considerably since she returned home from work that day, making her consider going back inside. Instead, she chose to settle in the nearest deck chair and watch the black sky above her. There was no moon, only millions and millions of other suns for her to gaze at.

After taking a drink, she raised her left hand above her head to peer at the stone she wore. It was dull in comparison to the stars, picking up trace amounts of the light that sifted out from the house. It had been the most brilliant thing she had ever seen the first time she laid eyes on it, on a night like this eight months earlier. He had proposed to her on bended knee, in the gardens at his parents' estate. The honesty and earnest in his heart had shone just as bright as the diamond, making her answer automatic. Now, as she held it in comparison to the stars, she shook her head. That man, whoever he was, was long gone.

She knew now what everyone else had suspected – he was a cheater. After living together for half of their engaged life, it didn't take a genius to figure it out. He left for the clinic at six every morning with a promise to be back at a reasonable hour – in the beginning he'd kept that promise every night. But as the weeks wore on he started returning home later and later, until Monday of the eleventh week, when he didn't come home at all. Her best friend Helen had advised her to leave him and sell the ring. But she loved him desperately, finding comfort and security with his promise of marriage. As they wore on into their seventeenth week in the house they barely spoke to each other, and hadn't made love in nearly a month.

It wasn't love, she thought harshly, vivid details of their intimacy assaulting her. It was sex; that was all it ever had been. Her young age had only allowed her one semi-serious relationship before this, with a high school friend named Elliott. The memory of lying together on his dorm room floor immediately brought a smile to her lips. They never went all the way, but instead used their nighttime sessions to explore aspects of themselves that they didn't yet know existed. The one thing that Mattie was sure of was that she had never experienced that kind of intimacy with the man she intended to marry.

A pair of headlights pierced the dark to locate the three-car garage on the other side of the house. There were no lights on outside, only the garage light that activated with a motion sensor. The slatted wood door rose slowly to admit the Jaguar, protesting when it was forced back down again.

John was exhausted, and the thought of Maria carrying his child was weighing heavily on him; he needed some time to quiet his mind before he tried to go to sleep.

He found the house mostly dark, and assumed that his fiancée was already in bed. So he headed out to the patio, wanting to lie out in the hammock for a while.

Mattie jumped at the sound of the glass door sliding open, turning away immediately when she saw who it was. It took him a moment or two to see that she was here and not in bed like he thought, and another couple to figure out what he would do next. "Hi," he said softly, casually slipping his hands into his pockets as he gazed out across their tree-lined land.

"You're late," she commented before taking another drink from her glass. The blown design was thin in her hand, and she had to force herself to relax her grip before it shattered. "Tough day?"

He nodded as he made his way to the hammock on the other side of the deck. "Uh huh." A grunt of effort put him up on top of the woven cords, and another stretched him out into a semi-lying position. "How was your day?"

"Same as always." Mattie set the glass down on the small table beside her chair, risking a look at him. The sight of him in a suit had always driven her crazy, and tonight was no exception. Before she knew what she was doing she found herself on her feet, slinking over toward him as her fingers involuntarily opened the top two catches of her dress. His eyebrows lifted in interest, and with a bit of coordination she climbed into the hammock to carefully straddle his hips before she kissed him. After all, that was what tonight had been for in the first place.

He licked away the saliva that she had left behind when they parted, his hands instinctively sliding up under the hem of her flared skirt. "What was that for?" he questioned.

She shifted her position, carefully setting herself down where she knew he would be most receptive. "No reason," she whispered, kissing at his neck as she started to loosen his tie.

"No."

The abruptness of the word caught her completely by surprise, forcing her back on her heels. "What?"

"Not now. I'm tired." With that he gently pushed her off of him and climbed down out of the hammock. Stunned, Mattie swayed gently in the breeze as she watched him go into the house.

Back in the city, a single light shone from an old garage on Lewis Street. Maria put the car in park and sank back into the driver's seat in utter defeat. A new barrage of tears started to stream down her face, blurring the image of the envelope that sat on the dash. She reached for it after a while, staring at the second ultrasound photo for a very long time. His child sat in her hands – the child that she wanted, but that she didn't want to raise alone. The child that, to him, meant disaster.

Eventually she reached up for the button on her visor and closed the garage door. She didn't realize when, but she started the engine again. She eventually dozed off, clutching the picture of her daughter to her heart as she faded away.

Chapter 3

Mattie's perfect view of her bedroom ceiling was jolted over and over again before her eyes squeezed tightly in an attempt to shut everything out. Above her John was doing what he usually did in bed, and the same moves that had enthralled her when they first met now only fuelled her boredom. She was aware of every thrust of his body, of the rasping in her ear and the rush that he seemed to be in to finish. He collapsed on top of her when he was done, and only then did her eyes open again. The sun was beginning to push through the heavy bedroom curtains, slowly forcing back the shadows that had filled the room only a few minutes before when he shook her awake.

His chin rested on top of her shoulder where it met her neck, the sharp bone digging just a little further in with every heave of his chest. She absently reached up to lay a hand on his back, reminding herself that she had spent the last few moments not showing him any sort of affection. Her fingers had just brushed his shoulder when he abruptly pulled himself off her and headed into the adjoining bathroom. For a moment or two Mattie was stunned, but the bathroom light came on and instead she opted to roll over and resettle herself under the covers, staring blankly at the wall that separated her from her fiancé.

When she was almost asleep again John stuck his head through the doorway, foam dripping off the end of the toothbrush that hung from his mouth. He didn't bother to remove it when he reminded her, "Don't forget – my parents will be here for dinner at six."

"Yeah," she mumbled, burying her face deeper under the comforter.

"And they hate eating late," he added before disappearing again.

She half sat up in order to protest. The sound of the shower being turned on ended all prospects of an argument, which would have started with who actually had punctuality issues. The only one that would pay any attention to her now was her pillow, and she wasn't about to disappoint it. But being aggravated by him now made sleep impossible. She rolled over, her eyes opening again to scan around the room.

The bright blue wrapper that sat on the edge of the nightstand made her stop and stare at the unopened condom. She kept them in the drawer underneath so that they would be in easy reach when they were needed, though more and more recently the package that was pulled from the drawer never made it off the white tablecloth.

John's younger brother had been married for five months, and his first niece was only a week old. Though John would never admit it, he was immensely jealous that he didn't have the same thing. He obsessed about it because Elliott was younger, and the way that John and Elliott were raised dictated that it was the oldest who got married and started their family first. So Mattie had become an unwilling participant of a strange game of one-upmanship, one in which she would pay the biggest price when John made any kind of offensive move.

The couple often clashed when their separate ideas about marriage came into play. Mattie's parents had been happily married twenty-eight years and had to contend with problems like bankruptcy and unemployment along the way. John's had been together for six years more, but it was easy for Mattie to see that their relationship was strained. John's father was deep in the throes of mid-life crisis, complete with self-help books and a suddenly endless bank account. His mother eagerly took on the role of family matriarch, quite content to have not only her sons, but also her daughters-in-law, tied to her apron strings.

The most unfortunate result of all of it was that John had absolutely no idea of what it was like to be in a relationship where he wasn't in complete control. Without question he expected her to change her name, stay at home and immediately start having children. When Mattie decided against all of those things, he went through the roof. She was proud of who she was and where she came from, so she refused to do what she saw as throwing that identity away just because she was getting married. Two days after they moved in together, she started a new job, which resulted in another round of fights.

The biggest point of contention came when she told him that they were going to wait two years after their wedding before they started trying to conceive a child. It was not something that John would take lying down, so the argument came up every time someone initiated sex. Sometimes she won and they used the condom, sometimes her wish to keep him happy won out. He had won this morning.

The water was turned off, allowing the sound of John's cough to be amplified by the shower tiles. With a huff she reached over and put the condom back in the drawer. She got up before he could reappear, grabbed her robe off the chair in the corner and headed down to the kitchen to make some tea.

Chapter 4

John was still thinking hard about what had happened with Maria the night before as he drove into town, and about how he had insisted on no condom that morning with Mattie. He felt badly for what he had said to Maria – he actually did want children, but he was afraid of how his family would treat him with a child out of wedlock. His brother and his wife had gotten pregnant while they were engaged, which caused a lot of tension with not only the brothers' parents but their grandparents as well. The fuss had been so strong that it caused the couple to move up their wedding date to ensure that the baby was born after they were married. Despite appearances, John was deathly afraid of disappointing others. But he wasn't afraid enough to wait until after he and Mattie were married.

Without a conscious decision, he found himself steering toward Maria's house rather than the clinic. He needed to apologize to her – he really had not meant to be as cruel to her as he had been. Entrapment wasn't like her. Deeply religious, it had taken a lot of convincing on his part just to get her into bed. A baby meant revealing their relationship to her family, which he knew she had also hidden because of the embarrassment of being the other woman.

His car slowed when he saw an ambulance and squad car parked outside her house. "What the…" He parked across the street and got out, then followed a series of voices until he found a crowd of strangers clustered around the opened garage door at the side of the house. Maria's car was still in the garage, the driver's door open. "Maria?" he called out, suddenly breaking into a run.

The nearest cop caught him before he could get close. "You can't go in there, sir," he warned, grabbing John by the shoulders and holding him back. "This is a crime scene."

"I'm a doctor," he told him, still trying to push past.

"We don't need a doctor," another officer said, helping his colleague direct John away from the garage. "Who are you?"

"Doctor John Frost. I'm her–" He stopped, not really sure what he was to her. Finally he said, "I'm her friend."

The cops looked at each other, then the first one said to him, "I'm sorry, Doctor Frost, but Maria Hawthorne is dead." They guided him to the back steps when his knees buckled, making sure that he was stable when sat down.

The coroner stood back up when he was finished, leaving Maria's body sitting behind the wheel for the moment. "I'm all finished here," he told the detective he was with.

"It's a good thing," she said, gesturing to the man on the back step. "I think her boyfriend just showed up."

Chapter 5

Helen Davidson's heart was pounding as she raced through the cramped hallways of the college's trades building toward the final exam that was awaiting her. The door was going to close in eight minutes, and it was on the other side of the machine shops. Her lungs were burning when she rounded the last corner into a window-lined hallway that would lead her to the right classroom.

She yelped when she connected with a solid body that was coming from the opposite direction, her pen flying from her hand as she got the wind knocked out of her. Helen was able to take in a few deep gulps of air before looking up to see what she had hit.

Kevin Delamont towered over her, his shocked expression mirroring her own. He reached up to readjust his black ball cap, running a hand over to smooth his hair before replacing the hat. She was the last person in the world that he ever would have expected to see – she had never returned his initial call after their meeting in the campus bar two weeks before. But now she was there, blonde hair askew from running into a more-or-less stationary object. It prompted him to smile. "Hi."

"Hi." Helen suddenly realized that her hair was hanging in her face and yanked the offending pieces back to tuck them behind her ear. A slight flush of embarrassment colored her cheeks, but he was too busy gazing at her to really notice it. She was momentarily at a loss for words, particularly when trying to remember his name. Finally she managed to come up with, "Keith, right?"

He frowned as he softly reminded her, "It's Kevin."

"Oh yeah." The redness in her face deepened, and Helen let out a nervous laugh. His curly brown hair stuck out a good inch on either side of his ball cap, thick and shaggy to match the unkempt beard that he wore. His tall, lanky frame was dressed in a button down plaid shirt and jeans, with boots that had obviously seen better days. She hadn't thought much of him when they met at the bar, but seeing him now, looking like he'd wandered in straight from the mountains, was beginning to change her mind. "How are you?"

"I'm good." His attention was taken away from her hair when he saw her deep green eyes, which were unintentionally staring back at him. She stood a head shorter than him and was painfully thin all over, her pastel T-shirt tightly tucked into a worn pair of jeans. These were accompanied by two dollar canvas runners which she had spent many class hours drawing on in a variety of colors. She looked exactly the same as she had in his daydreams over the past couple of weeks, which did nothing but further his interest in her. He offered his hand to her and asked, "Where are you off to in such a hurry?"

His question reminded her that there was an exam beginning any second without her. "Oh shit!" she swore under her breath as she clambered to her feet. Helen pushed past him to head down the hall, then stopped a few steps later when she realized that she no longer had a pen in her hand. Kevin was still staring at her, perplexed by her sudden attempt at departure. His brow furrowed deeper as he tried to figure out what it was she was looking for when she took slow, deliberate steps around him, staring intently at the floor. "Where is it?"

He looked around the dark tile floor, trying to follow her searching eyes when she passed him. "Where is what?"

"My pen." The pitch in her voice was rising with every unfruitful second. "I've got an exam starting right now."

Kevin quickly glanced around but couldn't see what she was looking for. So instead he reached into his shirt pocket and offered his. "Here – take mine."

She heard him say something, but she was so intent on finding her pen that the words didn't register. "I can't miss this," she worried as she continued to look.

He reached over and touched her shoulder to get her attention. "Here," he said again, holding his pen out for her to take. "Take mine." Helen was hesitant, and he pushed it just a little closer toward her. "Go on, take it." With a smile he added, "I don't have any exams today."

After a moment's consideration she took the pen, careful not to touch his fingers in the process. It held her attention for a moment, then she looked up at him and said, "Thanks." Their eyes locked once more, and then she dashed down the hallway, where the exam monitor already had her hand on the doorknob.

Kevin watched until the door shut, a bemused grin crossing his face when he turned around to continue on his original route. With a snap of his fingers he remembered that he had been carrying a cell phone at the time, so now it was his turn to search the floor. The phone had landed a few feet away, stuck halfway underneath a door. A bright flash a small distance from it caught his attention, belonging to a gold plated pen. He remarked to himself how it had just happened to be there for him to find, then tucked it into his pocket and dialed his brother's number again.

Mattie reveled in the early morning sunshine, warming her through her thick robe as she walked back from the mailbox. A few bills, a card from John's aunt and a flyer for a local drug store made up the material that she flipped through. A plain white envelope with a scrawled address caught her attention, but she waited until she was back in the hammock before setting down everything else and tearing it open. A grin filled her expression the instant she started to read the letter, dated a week before it had arrived.

Dear Matt,

Things here are crazy, so I'm taking a study break before my brain explodes. My finals are in a week, and then I'll be done my first year of college. I'm beginning to think that I'm never going to be finished.

Allison dragged me out to the bar last Friday – completely against my will as usual. She introduced me to her husband's friend, a guy named Kevin. He seems nice enough, but can't dance to save his life. Slow songs he's okay with, but if you request a fast song you're taking your life into your hands. He called me on Tuesday but got the machine because I was still in class. I'm not sure if I really want to call him back. Allison is already mad at me because I haven't had three dates with him yet. Well, just because she got married when she was sixteen doesn't mean the rest of us have to.

Well I suppose I should get back to work. I'll call you as soon as I get into town – I should be home by the second week of May latest. I've been dying to go to West Ed for months now.

Talk to you soon,
El

Mattie flipped the single page over, finding the random scribbling and cartoon drawings that Helen always enclosed with her letters. There was one about a teacher from hell, and another depicting a geeky first date for Mattie. She laughed and thought to herself, *She hasn't even met John yet.*

As she continued to flip through the rest of the mail another envelope fell into her lap, which had been hidden away inside the flyer. There were no addresses of any kind, only a single line with her name on it. Mattie held it up to the sun to try and gain a clue to its contents, then opened the letter and picked up her mug again.

As her steely blue eyes started scanning the handwriting, she brought the mug to her mouth to drink. The warm ceramic surface rested against her bottom lip, but no liquid washed inside. The letter had her full attention now. It detailed every bit of information about an affair that the good doctor had initiated three years before, which had continued well past his official engagement photos without any signs of slowing down. It listed all of the things that he loved to do during sex, proof that this was not just some random woman who was attempting to blackmail him.

Mattie absently reached to set her tea down, so completely absorbed by the letter that she didn't realize where she was. The mug shattered on the cobbled terrace, but she didn't notice. She read the same line, over and over again. Her breath quickened, pressure building in her chest as she tried to accept what she had just learned. She continued to read it until the tears in her eyes blurred everything beyond recognition.

Chapter 6

Mark Layton awoke with a start, his eyes barely cracking open as he pounded on the alarm clock. With a sigh he buried his cheek back into the pillow, instantly drifting into the dream he had just left. But the ring was insistent, trying to pierce the fog in his brain. He hit the alarm again, this time leaving his hand over it to see if it would go off again. When the ring came a third time he finally managed to put two and two together, so he reached for the phone on the nightstand instead. "Hello?" he grumbled, laying his head back down and covering it with the receiver and his arm.

"Mark?"

His lack of patience was clear. "Yeah, what?"

"Mark, it's Mom."

A layer of sleep peeled away. "Mom?" He reached over and grabbed up the clock, which read five after six. His mother had a habit of calling him early in the morning, the only time she could reach him since he was hardly ever home. It was also designed as a bit of fun, an attempt to catch him in the middle of something – but she hadn't done it in over a year. "Why are you calling me so early?" he grumbled, setting the clock back down and picking up the phone's base as he sat up in bed.

There was a long silence on the other end of the line. "Maria is – is dead."

The phone's base dropped through his fingers, tumbled off the edge of the mattress and clattered onto the hardwood floor. The noise awoke Sasha beside him and prompted his beloved golden retriever Jack to suddenly sit up between their feet. "What do you mean dead?" he quietly demanded.

The minute that his mother started to tell him what happened, she started sobbing. "There was...there was an – an accident..." she stammered.

"Oh Jesus," he gasped, his head falling back against the headboard.

"We have to...to..." This time she broke down into uncontrollable sobs, so hard she couldn't breathe anymore.

"It's okay," he told her, pretty sure that there would be no more conversation right now. "I'll be there as soon as I can, okay?" There was no answer. "Mom?" The phone clicked in his ear as she hung up, but not before he heard her burst into tears again.

Mark reached over to put the phone back on the receiver, now realizing that the base of the phone was on the floor. He slowly pulled it up by the cord, put the entire unit back together and placed it on the table. Sasha was sitting upright now, her eyes examining him. She softly asked, "What happened?"

Though the news had not sunk in, he answered in a hollow voice, "My sister is dead." He flipped the covers back off his legs and went into the bathroom. Jack got down off the bed and followed him, reappearing in the doorway a few seconds later. He looked from Sasha to Mark and back again, unsure of where he should be at the moment. "I have to go to home."

Sasha pulled the comforter up closer to her chin, her bare shoulders suddenly rippling with goose flesh. She had only met Maria once, when she was invited to his family's home for Christmas the year before. Sasha found her pleasant enough, though deeply troubled. Mark's girlfriend never paid it any mind because she didn't really care for any of his family – his siblings or his parents. "Do you want me to come with you?" she asked, knowing she had to. But there was absolutely no sincerity in the question.

In the bathroom, Mark had been staring at his own reflection in the harsh light. The sharp tone of her offer caught him off guard, prompting him to go back out into the bedroom. He stopped just short of Jack, who lifted his head to request some attention. "What?"

"I'll go with you if you want me to," she repeated, absently pulling at the folds of the blanket.

"But *only* if I want you to," he taunted.

She fixed him with a cold stare. "Just what is that supposed to mean?"

He stared at her in disbelief. "Jesus Sasha, my sister is dead!"

Her glare never wavered. "Do you want me to go with you or not?"

"No," he told her before he'd really decided. At his side Jack pushed his master's hand with his snout, but still didn't receive any attention.

He barely heard her when she said, "Fine." The pair glared at each other for a split second more before he went back into the bathroom. She kicked off the blanket and rushed over to the pile that her clothes had been dumped into the night before.

Mark was once again staring into the mirror when he heard the front door slam shut. He lost track of how long he stood there, only brought back into reality when Jack's nose pressed up against his bare thigh. With a shake of his head he sat down on the edge of the closed toilet seat. Jack came over and rested his jaw on Mark's knee, his eyebrows dancing as he looked to his master for an explanation. Mark scratched absently behind the dog's ears as tears started to roll down his cheeks.

John's car pulled into the garage at about five-thirty that afternoon, a small screech emanating when he put it into park without completely stopping first. The door to the rest of the house was locked, with no deadbolt or lock that he could open with his keys. Grumbling, he went back through the garage door and around to the front entry. There to greet him were all of his clothes, thrown mercilessly in one great pile that spilled off the grass and onto the sidewalk. He ran for the door, finding it locked as well. When he finally did find his key, he was only able to push it about halfway into the lock before it was obvious that it was not the correct one. "Mattie!" he shouted, frustration making him press down on the decorative door handle again. "Mattie, open up!"

In the master bedroom, Mattie was busy tearing all of her fiancé's suits from their hangers. He was meticulous about his clothes, most of the trousers hanging upside down in large wooden clips. She wrenched each pair so hard from the hangers that some of the red felt lining was torn off the wood with them. There was a sizable pile at the foot of the bed, so each additional piece that she threw at it tumbled down onto the carpet. He had called her several times before she actually heard him, and with her anger escalating she slowly walked over to the large window.

For a moment she watched him through the sheer white curtain. He would give up pounding on the door to stalk back to examine the damage she had inflicted on his belongings. John would find a broken personal item, then race back to the door to try and get in again. He did it twice before looking up to the window, where he managed to spot her face. "Mattie!" he hollered. "Mattie! Open the goddamn window!"

She did as she was told, completely cranking the pane outward before realizing that she had just followed a command. Inwardly she cursed herself for it – outwardly, she cursed at him. "What the fuck do you want?" she spat, taking advantage of the distance between them to rise up to her full argumentative potential.

John pointed to all of the stuff out on the front lawn, his voice rising again when he demanded, "What the hell is this?"

"You're moving out!" was her reply.

He frowned. "What are you talking about? Get down here and open this door!"

Her arms defiantly folded across her chest. "No."

John's mouth opened to shout his demand, to hurry her to the front door. Her response caught him completely off guard, and for a moment his jaw was left hanging. "Wh – what?" he stammered.

"I said no!" Mattie watched him again, this time satisfied with the situation that she had forced him into.

"Mattie, let me in!" he called, his tone beginning to shift toward desperation. For a moment he waited, but exploded when her face disappeared from the window. "Mattie! For Christ's sake Mattie, get down here and let me into my own goddamn house!" After a few moments she returned to the window, this time carrying most of the clothes that had been piled at the end of the bed. She started to hurl things down at him. "What the hell are you doing?"

Her heart was beating wildly in her chest now that the opportunity to tell him had arrived. All day she had thought about what to say when he asked her that particular question. "What I should have done a long time ago!" she yelled at him.

For a little while he was lost for words and still unable to believe that this was really happening. Mattie had so nicely fallen into place once they moved in together. This was completely against her nature. What didn't occur to him was what might have set her off. "What the fuck is your problem?"

She disappeared from the window again, and this time when she came back, she hurled a crumpled ball of paper toward him. It fell down into the bushes along the front of the house, and he trampled through the flowers beneath them to retrieve it. His face went ashen when he read the handwritten letter. "Why don't you just go move in with your whore!" she screamed down at him.

"Don't you call her that!" He exploded as soon as she had used the word, the letter crushed in his hands. All his anguish at the loss of Maria erupted to the surface. "Don't you ever call her that!"

"I don't believe you!" Mattie started to preach from her elevated position. "You won't apologize for cheating on me, but you're going to defend her?"

He fixed her with an unflinching stare. "I never cheated on you!"

Later on, Mattie would find it ironic that she chose that particular moment to start laughing. She challenged, "Oh really? So how did she get pregnant?" Mattie had tolerated about as much as she cared to, and she started to crank the window shut.

He looked up to see the window closing. "Mattie! *Mattie!*"

The window frame came back and sealed airtight, cutting off most of the sound of his voice. Her fingers were shaking when they left the handle, lifting up to cover her face when she burst into tears for the sixth time that day. On the window seat in front of her was her open package of cigarettes, which she reached for when she finally settled down again. As the smoke filled her lungs she kept staring through the sheer curtain, watching him losing his temper down on the ground.

He could still see her face in the window, which angered him even more. He shouted and cursed at her until he was hoarse, and all the time she never stopped watching him. At his wit's end and unable to enter his home, he demonstrated a choice selection of sign language before going back to his car to flee.

As she flipped through the exam to make sure that she had at least attempted to answer all the questions, Helen felt a great deal of pressure lifting off her shoulders. She had missed one on the third page, so she folded the preceding pages behind it and took the time to consider an answer. A piece of a song filtered into her brain, but she forced it back and made herself concentrate on the problem. Her eyes closed as she thought, and after a few moments the solution came to her. She slowed her writing speed to ensure that whoever marked it would be able to read it, then as soon as she could she handed it in and bolted from the room.

She headed directly outside into the sun and fresh air that was her favorite part of the campus grounds. A glance at her watch told her that she had about twenty minutes before she had to meet Allison back in their dorm room, so she settled down on a shallow, grassy slope to soak up some sun. She sighed as a fresh breeze blew across her body, the ground beneath her remarkably dry for April. Winter had been far too long for her, and she was basking in the opportunity to be outside without layers of survival gear. She briefly reviewed the exam in her head, but then forced herself to let it go.

Kevin Delamont's image floated through her thoughts as she lay there, and she tried to remember anything that they may have talked about the night they met. The only thing she remembered was that Allison was beyond excited to introduce the two of them. It was one of the qualities that Helen truly despised in her roommate – her love for matchmaking. It had not been the first time that Allison tried to fix her up with someone, so Helen had gone into the meeting with a jaded attitude and never had given him a second thought.

When a shadow blocked out her glorious sun, Helen's eyes flew open to find Kevin's image still floating above her. When it didn't disappear, she let out a squawk of surprise not unlike their first meeting that day, and scrambled to get out from underneath him.

"Sorry," he quickly apologized, a pacifying hand reaching toward her as he crouched down. "I didn't mean to scare you."

"That's okay," she assured him as she sat up, feeling her racing heart starting to slow down. "I'm...surprised to see you again so soon."

"I just happened to see you leave the building." He rocked back until he was sitting on the grass, the slope of the hill cutting the distance which he had to travel down. When he saw the look on her face he grinned and said, "I'm not stalking you, honest."

Helen found that she was scowling and consciously forced herself to relax. His pen was still in her hand, unconsciously turning in her fingers. When she saw him watching it she blushed, then handed it over. "I should give this back to you."

"Thanks." He pulled the plastic cap off the blunt end and placed it over the tip before putting it back into his shirt pocket. His fingers brushed over the gold pen, which reminded him to give it back to the young woman. "I think this is yours."

"You found it!" she exclaimed as she snatched it out of his callused hand, turning it over and over to check for any damage. "Where did you find it?" He explained where he had spotted it, and she couldn't stop grinning when she said, "Thank you."

After a while he commented, "Must have been someone special."

Helen was broken from her thoughts, frowning again when she looked up at him. "I beg your pardon?"

Kevin grinned again. "I mean this," he told her, gesturing toward the pen. "It must have been someone special who gave it to you."

She was quickly becoming entranced by his charismatic smile and his attention to detail. "It was my grandfather," she informed, once again turning her attention to the pen in her hands. "He gave it to me a week before he died."

He readjusted his position beside her when sitting on the slope gave him a shooting pain through his lower back. "You were pretty close, huh?"

"Yeah," she nodded. "He practically raised me." Helen caught herself, realizing that she was divulging too much information to someone that she really didn't know. Her watch was conveniently close, so she rotated her arm to get a look at it. "I gotta get going," she lied, using the excuse to get up onto her feet. "Thanks for the pen."

He was stunned, once again finding her in a rush to run away from him. He hurriedly called after her, "Can I call you?"

She stopped to think for a moment, then turned around and crossed the distance back to him. His hand fit comfortably in hers when she grabbed it and turned it upward, gold pen flashing as she wrote her parents' number down on his palm. "I'll be there in a week," she told him. "You can call me after that." With her pen tightly clutched in her hand, she took off toward the dorms, leaving him sitting there in the warm sun.

Chapter 7

Mark checked his rear view mirror, now noticing the dark blue sports car that was quickly closing the distance between them. He glanced down at his speedometer and confirmed that he was still doing thirty over the speed limit. By his estimate, the other car was doing at least twenty faster than he was.

Jack's feet twitched as he slept on the reclined passenger seat beside him. Mark reached over and scratched him behind the ears, then turned his attention back on the highway in front of him.

Wind roared past the small crack in the other car's driver-side window, the difference in pressure sucking ashes off the end of the cigarette that was held to it. The interior was filled with music, as loud as the stereo could possibly crank it out. Graham Martin's eyes were alternately occupied with watching the road and tossing his cigarette out the window. Once the filter was gone and he could close his window again, he readjusted himself in his seat and did a couple of head rolls to stretch out his neck and back.

The trip out to the coast had been a lousy one, mostly because of the fact that he spent all of his time alone. His breakup with Kim had been harder on him that he was willing to admit, but his brother's advice to take some time away from everything was well heeded. He went back to many of the places where his parents had taken him as a child, most of them on Vancouver Island. He had hoped that revisiting places that held fond childhood memories would help him feel better. At first it had worked, but the success had only been marginal. After three days of self-induced seclusion at Long Beach, he came to the realization that he was just fooling himself – that being there was not going to help him in any way, shape or form.

He was heartbroken. What made it worse was knowing that while he was at the beach trying to find some solace, she was back at their house moving her things out. He couldn't bear the thought of watching her pack up and leave after living together for nearly three years. But forcing himself to be away felt like all the times during university when he had no choice but to hang out at the library because his roommate was having sex with his flavor of the week. He detested every second of it.

His frustration mounted, so rather than keep himself in seclusion, he started heading back toward home, now racing through the long stretch between Kamloops and Jasper. Stopping only for gas, he'd managed to make it this far in record time, helped by the lack of traffic during the night.

Both cars, already significantly beyond the speed limit, started rushing up a steep incline. Graham's vehicle was only inches behind the other, forcing Mark to stomp on his accelerator to maintain a safe distance. Graham was driving on autopilot, so wrapped up in his own misery that he automatically matched speed. After a few moments he swerved into the oncoming lane, trying to take the lead.

Mark risked a glance at the other driver as Graham's car pulled alongside his. The man was pale, with large circles under his eyes and shoulders that looked like they carried a very heavy burden. It was all the observation he got; out of the corner of his eye, he spotted the oncoming logging truck.

"Oh fuck!" He slammed on his brakes, pulling to the right as far as he possibly could while still having some control. Gravel spit in all directions when he hit the narrow shoulder, the front passenger tire actually resting in the sparse grass beside the road. His knuckles were white around the steering wheel, breath heaving in his chest as he watched the blue car effortlessly move back into the proper lane. Jack had been startled out of his slumber and was anxiously looking around for what caused it, and once Mark noticed this he reached over and gently massaged his ears. "It's okay, pal," he said, more to soothe himself than anything. "You're okay."

Graham hadn't even noticed the threat to his life until he actually passed it, and then only because the volume of the heavily loaded truck buffeted his vehicle sideways. For a moment he thought that the truck would have done him a favor by killing him, but it was a fleeting notion.

He finally decided to take a break when he reached a lookout area, hitting the brakes hard enough to make the tires squeal. Freshly-lit cigarette in hand, he stretched his legs as he wandered along the stone wall that fenced the area from the valley below. The early morning air was brisk, turning the moisture in his breath into a light fog when he exhaled. Idle curiosity made him read the sign that explained the point of interest, and when he tired of reading, he turned to look out at the mountains that towered up in every direction. They seemed to be a living creature, standing down in judgment of him. He wished that the cradle they formed would swallow him up and end his agony.

He was so embroiled in his own thoughts that he didn't notice a motorhome pull into the scenic vantage point. A family of six poured out of the vehicle, complete with giggling kids and parents trying to keep a handle on their running brood.

Graham glanced back at them over his shoulder, feeling the usual revulsion that accompanied the arrival of children. He felt the distinct need to distance himself from them, returning to his car before the kids could reach him. But concentrating on scanning the terrain failed to drown out the growing level of noise, the children's laughter only reminding him that this sight, which had awed him when he was a young boy, now served to remind him of just how lonely he was.

He stood there long after the motorhome had left, but the awe never returned.

Chapter 8

Helen and Mattie had a long-standing tradition of being weird in public. One of their favorite pastimes was going for coffee in well-attended restaurants; they would order coffee with fries and gravy, and then start acting out lives that never belonged to them. Usually it revolved around a fantasy life in which Mattie was a hugely successful movie star and Helen was her tough-as-nails agent. A game they played since meeting as teenagers, it was a practice that usually managed to empty all the tables that surrounded them within an hour or two.

But that was all put aside, as they had been separated for almost a year and Mattie was in no mood for playing games. Since the breakup she had been miserable, constantly reviewing things over and over in her head to see where she and John had gone wrong. In her mind she would boastfully tell herself that it had been all his fault – that he deserved the small amount of damage that she had managed to inflict on his belongings before she left. The voice inside her refused to believe any of it; instead, it constantly reminded her that it really was all her fault and that she didn't deserve to start feeling any better.

Mattie hugged her tightly when she finally showed up at the restaurant, reveling for a moment in the comfort of seeing her best friend. Quickly pushing her emotions aside, she held Helen back at arm's length to get a look at her. "You look fantastic!"

"Goddesses always do," the other countered, flipping her hair back in melodramatic fashion. Then back to normal she said, "You're the one who looks great." Helen squinted as she scrutinized her friend. "You've gone down a couple of sizes, haven't you?"

Mattie nodded as they sat down, saying, "It's amazing what happens when you don't want to eat." While Mattie was reaching for her napkin, she couldn't help but notice the easy, laid back manner that Helen now had. "So what's new?" she opened.

"Oh, not much." Helen spread her own napkin across her lap and turned her coffee cup upright. "I did pretty well on all my exams." With dramatic flair and an evil grin she added, "And now I'm off for the next four months!"

Mattie rolled her eyes. "Oh shut up." She silently watched the woman on the other side of the table, her eyes scanning every detail about her. Her hair had lengthened, and the lines that extended from the corners of her eyes had stretched a little further outward. Other than that she was still the same old Helen, in a much better mood than usual.

Helen returned the scrutiny, not quite sure of what had captured her friend's attention. Mattie herself had thinned considerably since they saw each other last, taking great pains to make changes in her overall appearance. Her makeup had streamlined, while the curly bob that her hair was usually worn in had straightened and been shortened to almost non-existent. Helen started to feel uncomfortable under Mattie's eyes. "What?"

"Nothing." Mattie adopted a carefree, yet curious attitude as she turned her own cup over. "You just look like a woman who has someone to occupy their mind."

Her friend's jaw fell open. "What makes you say that?"

Mattie laughed. Helen had always been quite transparent. "Because I've never seen you quite like this before. I figure either you're in love or you've won the lottery. Now who is he?"

The waitress came by and filled their cups, promising that she would be back in just a minute to take their orders.

"I told you about him in my last letter," Helen said. "Allison introduced me to him."

Mattie tried to remember reading the letter, but with it arriving on the same day as the letter from Maria Hawthorne, she just couldn't recollect what Helen had said. "What's his name again?"

"Kevin." Helen reached for a packet of sugar, deciding that she didn't want to start talking about how happy she was when her friend was obviously in pain. Mattie was not nearly as open with her emotions, but Helen had a special insight into her friend. "So how are you doing?"

Mattie drew in a deep breath, enough to pull her shoulders up for a moment. "I'm okay."

Helen's spoon had been making a considerable amount of noise as she stirred the sugar into her drink. "Really?" she asked skeptically, the noise stopping abruptly.

"No," Mattie admitted, "not really." She poured cream into her coffee as she spoke, her eyes remaining fixed on the beverage's change from black to brown. "It's been hell untangling everything. He tried to have me pay for half of all the bills from when we were living together, he came in and took back all the gifts he'd ever given me…" She thought about the weekend she had returned to her parents' house to seek some sympathy, only to come home and find that he had managed to get in and take back the gifts, leaving glaring holes in shelves and on walls where Mattie had proudly placed them.

"Did you move out of the house?"

"I had to. I couldn't afford it." She reached for her own sugar. "And I've spent weeks returning wedding gifts that I never wanted to begin with." She sighed. "There were a lot of things that I never wanted."

Helen glanced around the restaurant, feeling some discomfort in discussing a topic that she really had no base of reference for. "What do you mean?"

Mattie stirred the sugar into her cup. "Well, at first, John seemed to be just a great guy." She took a sip, grimacing at both the bitter taste and the temperature. "It wasn't until we moved in together that I realized what kind of man he was," she said as she poured in more sugar. "He expected me to stay at home and take care of his house and his kids, and have his dinner on the table at seven o'clock when he got home from work."

Helen's eyes widened. "But you don't have any kids."

The other shook her head. "No. But I had a scare right after he moved out." She heaved a sigh, snatching her purse off the seat beside her to retrieve her cigarettes. "I never thought he would be the kind to cheat when I met him."

"Oh my god." Helen's expression twisted with horror and revulsion. "Who is she?"

"His best friend." Mattie set the pack down on the table and tried her drink again, finding it acceptable enough to take a long sip from the cup. "Apparently they were sleeping together long before he ever met me."

Helen tried to wrap her mind around the concept. "So he never stopped screwing her the entire time?"

"Nope."

Helen gaped at her friend, who had never made any mention of John's infidelity in the letters she sent during their college-induced separation. "How come you stuck around for so long?"

The waitress finally came back with a pen and a notepad, interrupting their conversation. "I'll have fries and gravy," Mattie told her, finally pulling out a cigarette and lighting it.

"Me too," Helen agreed. The waitress left them alone again, but Helen would not drop the subject. The way that her friend's demeanor changed at the mention of the breakup made it obvious that she had not really talked it through with anyone. So she prodded, "You were saying..."

Mattie pursed her lips, wishing that Helen would have forgotten what they had been talking about. "I don't know really," she said. "Everybody around us whispered about it, but nobody ever actually said anything. I guess I thought that if I ignored it, it wasn't really happening. And it was so much easier to be with him some of the time than to be alone." She took in a long pull of smoke, and heaved another sigh as she blew it out. "That all changed when I got the letter from her. It told me everything – how long they'd been together, all the things that he liked to do in bed, that she was five months pregnant – all of it."

Helen's coffee cup was halfway to her mouth when she heard the last part, and the cup hit its saucer with a ceramic bang. "She was pregnant?"

Her friend barely nodded. "But she died the night before I read the letter. Asphyxiated. The cops think that she drove out to our house to put the letter in the mailbox, then drove home and purposely closed the garage door behind her."

For a few seconds Helen was unable to find her voice. When she did, all she could do was gasp, "Wow."

Mattie's coffee cup rolled between her hands, warming palms that had suddenly gone cold. Her face was hot with emotion, the sting of tears beginning to fill her eyes. "I don't know how it happened," she softly said. "We went from being in love to being strangers within six weeks."

Helen remained silent to allow her friend to vent, who continued on when she said, "I thought that he was the one…" She heaved an uneven sigh, once again sliding into her own guilt. "Maybe I brought it all on myself. Maybe I should have just kept my mouth shut…"

"Stop that," Helen told her, reaching forward and putting her hand on Mattie's arm. "You don't deserve it. Nobody does."

Mattie gave her friend a sad smile. "I know I'm better off without him," she thought aloud, "but I just can't help but feel stupid, like it was all my fault."

Helen watched her friend, her heart constricting when she saw this woman – who very rarely cried – quickly approaching tears. "Don't ever think that," she advised. "You didn't do anything wrong."

A stray tear rolled down her cheek, and Mattie seemed angry at its escape as she swiped it away with the heel of her hand. "Then why does it feel like it?"

Helen got up and walked over to the other side of the table to hug her friend tightly. "I don't know, Matt."

Chapter 9

Dark, gloomy music filled the church seminary, organ notes reaching up and echoing off the vaulted oak rafters. Mark sat in the second pew on the far right side of the balcony, painfully aware of its unforgiving wooden structure under him. From his secluded vantage point he could see his mother, seated in the first row of the main section, with her daughter's casket only a few feet away from her. She was being tightly held by his stepfather on one side, and by his oldest brother on the other. Both had tried to get him to sit with them, but Mark refused to be anywhere near the coffin.

As the service wore on, he found himself recalling childhood memories, particularly revolving around the church that he had been a member of since birth. He had spent countless hours in the building, whether in Sunday school, youth groups or services. One of his earliest memories was hiding underneath the pews during Easter services when he was four, running into his twin when she had come up with the very same idea.

Mark and Maria had been extremely close, the best of friends. They confided in one another, fought occasionally and talked on a daily basis even though they lived in different provinces. She had left to attend nursing school in Edmonton when she was nineteen, and he moved west to Vancouver a year later to get his degree in business and start his career in advertising. But even living in different cities couldn't drive a wedge between them.

He had noticed a profound change in his sister three years before, when she started to date a doctor that she had met at a New Year's Eve party. The pair had fallen into a hard, fast relationship; Maria had described John as generous, driven and discreet, if not somewhat secretive. Being a very private person herself, he suited her. But John was secretive enough to keep his whirlwind courtship of Mattie Forrest from Maria until it was too late. The only other person she told about the baby was her twin, who she had sworn to secrecy. Even in death, her family had no idea she had taken another young life with her own.

Another bold chord from the organ jolted Mark from his thoughts, and his eyes soon rested on the centerpiece of the church. Her coffin was covered in a blanket of flowers – mostly carnations and a few lilies. The top was closed, allowing his tortured mind to try and believe that it wasn't for her. Identifying her grayed body in the morgue had been so shocking that he had mentally distanced himself from it. The only thing that did affirm her death was the fact that he hadn't received any calls from her. He was dying to tell her about the promotion at work that had finally come through, and about his breakup with Sasha. But as soon as he remembered that, he remembered what had prompted it. Once again the tears welled in his eyes, a few finally falling down onto his lap.

At the center of the church, the minister stepped out from behind his pulpit to lead the last hymn of the service. He looked down to the family that was seated in the front row, remarking to himself how much that family had changed since his arrival nearly thirty years before. When he delivered his first sermon there, he had noticed the stunning young woman who was seated in the front pew, her eyes intent enough to make him stumble through his words. To his dismay he discovered that she was engaged, but together they made the decision to become friends.

They still were good friends. Doris and Tom had watched each other get married and raise their families. It pained him to see her now, crying her eyes out and sitting through the formality of a church service that just put off the inevitable task of burying her only daughter. He made a mental note to pull her aside and talk with her later. "We now leave here to gather outside and commit our daughter, sister and friend to the earth," he announced, signaling the end of the service.

The pallbearers moved from their seats, taking a minute or so to get themselves organized before picking up the coffin. The flowered carpet shifted to one side, falling over the hands of the three men that held the brass handles. As they made their way back up the main aisle, her family fell into place behind them – all except for her twin. He lingered in the pew until he was the last person inside.

The parishioners were drenched by rain that had hardened since they went into the church an hour before. Most reached for their umbrellas, all but those who were too numbed by the funeral. Rain collected and streaked down Mark's cheeks, hiding the tears that he couldn't hold back. By the time he reached the grave, the casket was just being set on the fabric straps that would take it down. At the same time, Maria's mother stepped forward to readjust the flowers, to keep them from falling down into the empty pit below. The corner of Mark's lip curled slightly. Doris always had a habit of straightening anything that his sister wore.

The minister started into the final phases of the service. Mark tried to pay attention to what was being said, but found his attention constantly wandering from one face to the next. There were people here that he had known for years, and some that he didn't know at all. Unconsciously, he was making his way through the gathering to finally join his family, people parting to let him pass. A few stray pieces of sod littered the ground around the coffin, some wedged underneath the rounded metal frame that was holding it in place. He kicked one out from under the sole of his shoe as he stopped to stand behind his mother, his hand coming up to rest on her shoulder.

The minister threw a handful of dirt onto the flowers, some of it scattering onto the bits of polished wood that were exposed around them. A few people came forward to lay their own flowers, but Mark didn't twitch. His attention had been grabbed by a man on the other side of the grave. Mark didn't recognize him, but noticed the expensive suit that bagged around the stranger's hips as he made a last minute push forward to toss a full bouquet onto the casket. He was tall, meticulously kept – and heavily distraught. After a moment of contemplation he turned around and left, walking straight out to the parking lot on the other side of the church without looking back. Mark watched him until he disappeared around the corner of the building, then finally turned his attention back to the last time he would see his sister.

The minister thanked everyone for coming, then told them that there would be an open house at the Layton residence. The silence that had been constant all morning now was broken with subdued murmurs and the sounds of people walking across rain-soaked grass as they left. Mark spoke with his family, telling them that he would meet them back at the house and explaining that he had something he had to do first. He accepted the minister's condolences as he too departed, finally leaving Mark completely alone.

He now remembered the small item in his hand that he had been clutching all morning. In his palm was nestled a gold pendant, shaped like a baby's pacifier. The thin chain had been looped around his wrist twice to ensure that he didn't lose it, and as he stepped up to the edge of the grave, he removed it so that it dangled from the tips of his fingers. "Well, I guess this is it," he whispered to her. "I wanted to give you something before you go."

He lifted the pendant up to examine it one more time. The memory of his last conversation with her rushed back to him, and suddenly he felt the need to explain himself. "I know you said you were going to give the baby up for adoption, but I wanted you to have this." He started to cry again, a sob heaving in his chest. "I just wanted you to know that having that baby wasn't a sin. None of us were going to love you any less because of it." He took another step forward, close enough that he could rest his hands on the casket. "I thought you should have something to remind you of the great thing you were going to do for that couple."

His words faded into silence, the magnitude of his grief now finally hitting him full force. The tears blinded him to the world around the graveyard, and for what he thought was only a few moments he lost complete control. When he started to gather himself together again, he noticed that the undertaker and his assistants had returned and were waiting at a polite distance for him to finish. "I should get going," he told her softly, his hands trembling as they made their way down to the edge of the lid. It only lifted a couple of inches, far enough for him to get a glance of her hand. Mortal fear grabbed his heart, and he forced himself to reach inside and carefully coil the necklace into her half-closed palm. Once the lid was closed again he whispered, "I hope you like it."

He took a step back this time, turned and nodded to the funeral directors. In the few seconds before they reached him, he assured his sister, "Your secret is safe with me. I promise." The three men came, and one reached down to switch on the motor that started the coffin on its descent. Mark waited until it had been slowly cranked down into the ground, then finally tore himself away to return to his parents' house.

Chapter 10

Most of the shopping complexes and office buildings in downtown Edmonton were linked by a series of pedways, allowing shoppers and workers to travel from one building to next without actually going outside. Three separate buildings were attached together in an 'L' shape – the southwest being a shopping complex, the northwest an 18-storey office building and the east another shopping and office complex with one of the main bus stops on its east sidewalk. Mattie spent the majority of her days in the office building, where she had been working since she and John moved in together. She had to make her way over to catch the express that would take her back to her new home on the south side of the city, so when five o'clock rolled around she strapped on her snow boots, folded her long coat over her arm and headed for the bus stop.

Edmonton Center, the eastern shopping complex, was built in a cube shape; the stores were lined along the outside walls, and the center was a large, open area that housed the escalators for each floor. Mattie was riding the escalator down to the first floor when she heard someone calling her name. Above her, also descending, was Graham Martin. She had met him back in January, when she tried her hand at community theater. They had hardly said ten words to each other then – Mattie had never really thought much of him. As she looked up at him now, she thought about walking on as if she hadn't heard him. But he was making an effort to catch up with her, and she had been taught to be polite. So she stepped off the escalator and waited.

Graham waded through the mass of people that were filling the distance between them. He hadn't intended to be downtown when five o'clock hit, but the job interview he had been at ran late. She was standing a few steps back from the bottom plate of the escalator, the coat over her arm hiding the hands that were clasped together at her waist. Stuck at the very top by a solid pack of workers going home, he took the opportunity to get a good look at her. Her hair was much shorter than he remembered it, and she had gained a noticeable amount of weight as well. She was dressed in stereotypical office garb – a little too baggy, and really not that flattering – and her expression was enough to tell him that he was the last person on Earth she had expected to see.

Between the time that he last looked at her and when he looked up from the moving steps, she had pasted a convenient smile on her face. "Hi there," he greeted warmly.

Her response was flat and non-committal. "Hi."

He was unconscious of his own effort to keep a good distance from her, but as soon as he'd said hello, he'd picked up on her extreme caution. "How are you?" he asked.

For a split second Mattie thought about laying the whole story of her broken romance out for him, but with the slightest shake of her head dismissed it. "I'm alright," she finally told him. "How about you?"

"Not too bad, I guess," he said. "What are you doing downtown?"

"I work in the next building over," she told him, her left hand gesturing toward the west. "You?"

"I had a job interview. I was laid off three weeks ago," he explained.

She frowned, not sure of how to respond. She then settled for, "That sucks."

"Yeah." He looked around them, noticing that the crowd was starting to thin out. "What about you? How are the wedding plans?"

Her reaction to his question was hurried and abrupt, but in no way untruthful. "We broke up a few months ago."

"Oh. I see." He looked around uncomfortably as he thought. "You wanna go get some coffee?"

Mattie shook her head. "No, I have to be getting home."

After a moment Graham nodded, agreeing, "Yeah, I guess I should too." He started to leave, taking only a single step before he stopped. "You and I should get together sometime," he suggested, digging through his portfolio and handing her a page from it. "My phone number is on there. Why don't you give me a call sometime." Mattie looked at it for a moment, so he was compelled to explain, "I've had to move back in with my parents for a little while. But why don't you give me a call. We can maybe run through some music with the piano or something."

"Sure," she agreed, more to get him off her back than out of actual interest. "That sounds good."

"Great. I'll talk to you later then." This time he actually did leave, disappearing amongst the people that were still making their way out of the building.

Mattie examined the piece of paper he had given her and realized that it was the front page of his resume. One thing seemed to jump out at her – his date of birth. It confirmed that he was a decade older than she was. By the time she looked up again he was gone, so she folded the page up and tucked it into her purse, then put on her coat and headed outside toward the bus stop.

The ride from downtown to the south side took an hour, which gave Mattie's mind plenty of time to grind. She was still dwelling on how disastrous her breakup with John had been, and how ever since then she had sworn off men completely. Any optimism she had gained about dating since high school had been shattered by her ex-fiancé and, unintentionally, by Maria Hawthorne. But she had been given a few months to consider her position in her young life and, much to her own surprise, found herself thinking about Graham's offer.

When the two first met, it was amongst a group of twenty-five who were cast in a musical production for one of the local community theater groups. They were side by side in the crowd who stood below, adoring the queen on her balcony. The one thing that Mattie had noted about him was that, despite his enthusiasm, holding a note in tune could definitely be a challenge for Graham. And he was not exactly embraced by the younger members of the chorus who had become fast friends with. But she had started dating John around then, and never paid Graham any more mind.

Now she found herself imagining spending time with him and just generally getting to know him. *He isn't so bad looking,* she thought to herself. *What's it going to hurt to at least have coffee with him?* But before she could get very far into that train of thought, the bus slowed down to the stop nearest to her apartment.

Chapter 11

A blue Dodge pulled up onto the yard at her parents' cabin, the one vehicle that Mattie was dying to see. She couldn't go outside to meet them because she was already babysitting three of her friends in the kitchen, who were busy plotting their drunken escapades for the evening. Mattie turned away from the window and was immediately distracted by what her friend Carla was up to. "What the hell is that?" she questioned, pointing to the shot glasses that had been lined up on the counter.

"I'm experimenting," was the earnest response. "Maybe I should just forget this university thing and become a bartender."

Mattie took a closer look at the glasses. The bottom half of the drink was clear, and the top half was a bright blue liquid that had been carefully poured over it. "What's in it?"

"Blue Curacao and Long Island mix." Carla took a step back to admire her handiwork. "Let's drink."

The back door opened to admit Graham. "Hello?"

Mattie told Carla, "Don't drink yet." Then she went back into the porch to say hello to the newest party guests. "Hi," she told him, disappointment creeping into her expression when she saw only him standing there. "Where's Helen?"

"She's just getting her bag out of the car." To ensure some confidentiality, Graham took his friend by the elbow and leaned down to speak in her ear. "She's cute."

"She's got a boyfriend."

He was clearly disappointed. "Why is it you always introduce me to these friends of yours when they're already taken?" he asked, referring to another friend of hers. Graham had already been hitting on the curvy Elaine before finding out about her engagement, but stemmed his disappointment by accompanying Mattie to the wedding in order to take advantage of the free food and drink.

"To make sure you can't get your hands on them," she playfully jabbed, trying to see past him.

The door opened again, and this time Mattie's other best friend finally made her appearance. The pair hugged each other in greeting, and now Mattie knew that no matter what happened that night, she was going to have a good time.

"Come on, come on!" Carla moaned. "Are we talking or drinking?"

"Drinking!" the host confirmed as she skipped back into the kitchen, Graham and Helen following her. There were a dozen shot glasses, and her other friends Tony and Rob had now made their way into the kitchen from the patio door. Each one of them picked up a glass, Mattie turning and handing drinks to Helen and Graham. She wondered aloud, "What shall we drink to?"

Everyone thought for a moment, and then Tony was struck with recollections from the last party that Mattie had thrown. "I've got it. Here's to raging bulls and UFOs," he toasted, reminding everybody about the things that people had managed to see at the previous bash.

Everybody laughed, clinked their glasses together and gulped their drinks down. Air rushed out of their lungs with groans and whoops that people outside the house could hear. "Jesus Christ!" Helen gasped, slamming her shot glass back down on the counter as she tried to get her breath back.

"Well Carla," Mattie surmised once she stopped coughing, "I think you've found a replacement for sinus cleaner." She set the glass down and said, "Come on. Let's go get drunk."

A few hours later, a large crowd of twentysomethings were gathered around a raging bonfire in the middle of a small clearing beside the cabin. It was finally dark out, a clear field of stars over them with no moon. Rob had brought his car down so they could use his stereo, parking it a small distance from the fire. Benches circled the flames, formed by placing long planks across straw bales or five gallon plastic pails. The Forrest family's lakeside cabin was definitely a great place to throw a party.

Mattie spent the first couple of hours greeting and talking with people as they arrived, thoroughly enjoying herself. Her last party had been a smash, complete with her city-boy ex-fiancé and his brother going on a cow tipping mission, and both she and Carla spying lights in the sky that they had sworn were UFOs. She had been looking forward to letting loose here more than anybody, and at the rate she was imbibing, it wasn't going to be difficult.

After consuming a sufficient amount of alcohol, Mattie perched herself on one of the benches and decided to watch the people around her for a while. Just within a few feet of her were Les and Jennifer, yet another engaged couple. She couldn't help but let her eyes roll up into her head as they eagerly wrapped themselves in each other for a kiss. She loved them dearly, but they did seem to serve as a constant reminder that her prince had turned out to be a frog. "Alright, knock it off already!" she shouted at them before taking another swallow of beer. To make their point, the pair threw even more melodramatic passion into their embrace, each smiling with satisfaction when they heard the party's host wretch in disgust.

Graham plunked himself down beside her, bouncing the plank bench a little. He saw where her attention was focused and said, "So how's it going?"

Mattie sighed. "You know, there's days when I really hate those two."

"Well, what can you do?" he shrugged, gulping down some of his own drink.

"I don't know." She took a look at him. Half an hour before, she had witnessed the majority of the men heading out into the bushes, hurriedly talking amongst themselves with what passed for masculine giggling. And Graham had obviously been hiding something in the sleeve of his jacket. "I thought you were off bonding with the guys."

"We ran out of Sambuca." Graham shrugged again, his gaze wandering back across the crowd. "You seem to know an awful lot of strange people, Matt."

"Yeah," she confirmed. After a while she added, "Thanks for bringing Helen out."

"No problem. I like picking up strange girls."

She fixed him with a look, and just before taking another swallow of beer she told him, "I'm not even going to touch that."

The party really got into full swing with the arrival of a large number of theater people and, more importantly, two of her best beer buddies. Andi and Netta were both dressed in Caribbean-inspired outfits, and within only a few minutes of their arrival, they had drawn most of the group into their version of a ritualistic dance circle around the fire. Mattie joined in for a while, but gave up and headed for her beer when it became more like an exercise class. She found Rob nearby, so she sat down next to him to chat.

Graham watched the dance, shaking his head and wondering if his friends did things like that when they were this age. Then he remembered that his group were baked most of the time, so what they did probably beat these guys by a long shot. He decided to head back inside when nature called, and silently slipped away for a while.

Tony had just found out about Les and Jennifer's engagement that night, so he asked if he could take a look at the ring. "So have you set a date yet?" he questioned as he let go of her hand.

"November 15th," she said proudly as her fiancé wrapped his arms around her waist.

"You excited?"

"There's too much planning going on to be excited yet," Les told him.

Tony nodded. "Yeah. I guess that makes sense." Out of the corner of his eye he saw Graham walking toward them as he returned, not staggering but definitely not in a straight line. "How you doing?"

"Not bad, not bad." The pair of them shook hands. Graham asked, "When did you get here?"

Tony looked at him for a moment. "I was here when you got here, man."

Graham had to think hard before concluding that Tony was correct. "Oh right, I remember now." Then his attention was caught by something near the fire, and he said, "I'll talk to you later."

Mattie was still seated on the bench as she talked with Rob. She had turned sideways to face him, feet stretched out on either side of the plank. "So anyway," Mattie carried on with her work story, "I told him that if he wanted me to work all this overtime, that I'd want to take an extra..." Her voice trailed off when Graham snuggled up behind her and started to kiss the side of her neck. "...day off instead..." Rob and Mattie exchanged surprised glances, and then she gently asked Graham, "What are you doing?"

"Nothing." He pulled her closer to him and started to work his way up toward her ear.

Unsure of what to do, Mattie decided to carry on with her conversation. "What about you? I heard that you finally found a new job."

"Yeah, but it's no big deal," he admitted dejectedly. "I'm only working for my parents."

"But if they're paying you good money..." Once again she was distracted by the man behind her, who was now nibbling at her earlobe. For a split second she allowed herself to relish the moment, and then she half-turned to tell him, "You know, I'm going to need that back when you're done."

"Sorry," he apologized, pulling away just a little.

As soon as his lips left her skin, she was sorry she said anything. It surprised her. Mattie looked at him for a second, trying to read his mind. "Doesn't our office have a policy against this sort of thing?"

"Could be." In one swift motion, she felt herself being pulled into his arms, and was suddenly on the receiving end of a kiss like she'd never had before. One arm encircled her shoulders, and the other hand reached up to caress her cheek. For a moment the two of them became completely involved in one another, the world around them fading away until they were the only ones left. But as the seconds wore on they started to return to reality. The music from the car, the sounds of laughter and shouting, the crackling of the fire – everything came back one thing at a time. They still remained locked in the kiss, and to her amusement she heard Jennifer holler, "Hey! Knock it off!"

Distracted, Mattie's attention turned to the people around her. The party was still in full swing, but a few people had stopped to find out what was going on. She glanced at Jennifer in particular, who was wearing an expression that was a cross of amusement and apprehension.

Graham continued kissing at her neck, and when she turned back to him she lifted his jaw so that she could look into his eyes. Then with a devilish grin she pulled him down and kissed him hard, mostly to get a reaction out of her friends. And they didn't disappoint.

Chapter 12

Shopping was a necessary evil for Mark, one that he detested more than almost anything else in life. Especially grocery shopping. It was one of the things that, oddly enough, had managed to keep him from getting into any serious, long-term relationships – the fact that he was unwilling to set foot in a supermarket. He hated the congestion, the screaming children, the rude cashiers – all of it. The punishment for all this resentment was for him to live alone and shop for himself, and despite his own misgivings on the subject, his position was starting to soften. He still didn't like it, but at least now he didn't wait until a week after he'd run out of food before finally breaking down and going shopping rather than just ordering in.

He stood in front of a row of breakfast cereals, trying to decide what he really wanted to start his days with for the next week or so. Sugar bombs with pretend vitamins were what he had been raised on, and it was a habit that he had never been able to shake. Adult cereals full of fiber and goodness just never agreed with him, so he gave in to the inevitable and settled for the kids' fare. He had narrowed it down to three separate boxes when he felt something draw his attention to the other end of the aisle.

Sasha stood in profile, mulling over the few healthy breakfast choices that she favored. She also held a small, frost-laden container that she switched from hand to hand as she tried to make up her mind. But while her gaze flicked from one box to the next, an uncontrollable force pulled her toward the sugary selections that lined the rest of the shelves.

As soon as she saw him her eyes narrowed, and as she stared at him she wondered if it would be alright to talk to him. He had tried to reach her so many times after his sister's death, and she never returned any of his calls. Now Sasha didn't know what to do.

Mark solved her dilemma for her when he pushed his cart in her direction. It was clear by his speed that he had absolutely no intention of stopping, and she was quite content to let him pass. Her eyes followed as he strode by, head held high, his stare meeting hers for a split second before concentrating on his destination. He was nearly out of sight when she heard herself call after him in a stunted voice, "Hi Mark."

He stopped short, and as he slowly turned around she could see that his expression had changed from angered indifference to genuine surprise. He really hadn't expected her to say anything. From the depths of his amazement, Mark finally managed to find his voice and spit out, "S – Sasha...hi." They started at each other, then simultaneously burst into uneasy laughter. Uncomfortable, but brave enough to think he was completely over her, he asked, "So...how have you been?"

"I've been good," she nodded, readjusting the long coat that had slid halfway off her shoulder. Sasha looked at him for another moment. "You look great."

"So do you," he replied, surprised at the honesty in his remark. "Are you working near here?"

"No, I live just around the corner. Had a craving for chocolate ice cream, and..." She brandished the small container in her hand, "here I am."

Mark laughed, more freely this time. He felt at ease, and now regretted his defensive posture from a few moments before. He never could hold a grudge for very long. So to make it up to her he offered, "Listen, you wanna go get some coffee or something?"

Sasha took a moment to consider it. "Yeah," she finally said with a grin. "That sounds great."

The following Monday afternoon, Mattie was unwillingly parked at her reception desk, her chin propped up on her hand as she daydreamed about the party at the cabin. She kept going over the kiss again and again as she tried to figure out why it happened. She also was looking for the butterflies in her stomach that she had experienced that night, and every time she took her mind back to the moment, the butterflies returned. The fact that they had both been drinking never seemed to enter her mind – she at least knew that she had not been that far gone.

The telephone rang, and she nearly knocked over her water glass as she reached over to pick up the receiver. "Security Investigators…"

In his office, Graham was packing things up for the day. The deposit records went into the safe, the payables into the bottom right drawer in his desk. He collected his cigarettes and sunglasses, then made sure he had his keys and his jacket before stepping out into the reception area. He found Mattie just wrapping things up on the phone. "You ready to go?" he asked.

She nodded as she forwarded the lines for the night, then reached under her desk for her purse before standing up to take her coat off the back of her chair. Without a word she followed him out into the hallway, waiting when he turned around to lock the door. They had both discovered a definite shift in their relationship when they arrived at work that day. Once the door was locked and they started for the stairs down to the street, he offered, "Can I give you a ride to your car?"

A little distracted, she stumbled over her answer. "Y - yeah. Sure."

The block and a half ride to the small parking lot where Mattie's beat-up Mustang was parked was spent in complete silence. Even after Graham parked his car beside hers, they both sat there, saying nothing. Her heart was racing, and she tried not to let the heaving of her chest show her nervousness. There was so much on the line here, especially if he rejected her. She worked herself up in her mind, and with a tiny burst of courage she said, "Can I ask you something?"

Graham had been expecting something like this. "Sure."

Whatever courage she had managed to muster disappeared in the moment it took her to ask if she could ask a question. Ever since her breakup with John, her nerve had disappeared. Hesitation filled the small car's interior, and through tightened vocal cords she managed to whisper, "Are you...are...you..."

She had now confirmed his suspicions. "Am I interested in you?" He could see the breath she let out when he asked the question instead of her. Without any contemplation or thought he quickly said, "No." Her expression turned to one of not only disappointment, but also confusion as to how he reached his conclusion so fast. "What happened on Saturday night was...was..." He tried to think of the right way to phrase what he wanted to tell her. "Well, I don't know what it was. You're my friend, but to be honest, I've never been interested in you like that."

There was another pause – she couldn't believe that he had actually just said that. Heat flushed her cheeks, and a soft, "Oh," was the only reaction that she had. Not wishing to push the subject or embarrass herself any further, she reached for the door handle. "I'll see you tomorrow then." She got out, but stopped before closing the door just in case he had something soothing, or at least nice, to say. He just waited for her to go, his hands clutching the steering wheel in anticipation of getting home. She carefully closed the door behind her, then quickly got into her own car as he started to back away. For a while she sat there, staring into nowhere before she murmured, "You could have at least said you were sorry."

Chapter 13

Nearly a year passed by, giving Kevin and Helen just a few short months before they would graduate from their respective college programs. They spent their time doing typical couple things, such as window shopping for jewelry. The Saturday before Christmas, he made plans to take her to dinner at a moderately-priced chain restaurant.

The waiter, dressed in black pants and a bright green golf shirt, led them to the most secluded spot that they had left among the families and hollering children. Helen had barely sat down when Kevin ordered, "Give us a liter of the house red wine." The waiter nodded and quickly headed for the kitchen.

Helen's face screwed up slightly. "Red wine?"

"You'll like it," he told her, absently reaching for the card that listed drink specials.

Her eyebrows lifted briefly for a moment, but then she shook it off. "What's the occasion?"

"No occasion," he told her as he returned the drink card to its place behind the condiments. "I just feel like celebrating."

"Don't you normally have to have something to celebrate?" she asked absently as she read through the menu.

He shook his head. "Well if you must have a reason, I think that us getting married suffices. Don't you?"

She looked back up from the menu, fixing him with a funny look. "Yeah, I guess that will do."

"Which reminds me..." He dug into his jacket pocket to retrieve a black velvet ring box, which he haphazardly slid across the table at her.

"Is that the one?" she asked, picking up the box. A smile lit up her face when she saw what was inside, pleased but not surprised. "That's the one, alright."

He watched her as she pulled the ring out, hesitated for a moment, then slid it onto her own finger. "I'd have given it to you a while ago, but when I went to buy the ring you tried on, it had been sold. They ordered this one. I couldn't remember which one it was, so I had to guess."

"It's perfect." Helen took a moment to admire the small assortment of stones on her finger. "At least now my mother will think it's official."

The waiter returned with their jug of wine, and Kevin took it from him before it even hit the table. "Your mother loves me," he reminded her, reaching for his glass.

"She does." Helen sat back and watched him pour his own wine first, a feeling of contentment settling over her. This was the way it was supposed to be, not like the two other men she had dated in her lifetime. They had both gone out of their way to try and impress her with flowers and trinkets. One had even tried to serenade her outside her window until her father chased him off with a baseball bat. But Kevin was calm, intelligent, and never tried to embarrass her publicly. She liked his reserve – it suited her.

A smile curled her lips as she leaned across the table to kiss him. After all, a little public show of affection never hurt anyone.

Chapter 14

Dear Matt,

I'm so excited I don't know where to start. Kevin and I are getting married! It won't be for another year or so – it takes so long to get everything organized. In the meantime, he's taking a job back in Valleyview working construction, which is a great opportunity for him. Being long distance is going to suck, but it will be worth it in the long run. Eventually he'll move to Edmonton – but for now, moving in together sounds like a great idea. God, I can't wait – I'm so excited about everything.

You're going to be my maid of honor, right?

Gotta run. One more class and I'm done for the day. I'll talk to you soon.

Love,
El

In the year that had passed, despite the initial tension that existed between them, Mattie and Graham had settled down into a solid friendship and had become very attached to each other. Graham had held her at arm's length for a while, not wanting her to get the wrong impression of him.

He cursed the alcohol that led him to start kissing her that night, because he really was not attracted to her. He was still keenly aware of Kim's effect on him, which left him unsure of where he stood in his own life. Mattie had given him the cold shoulder at first, barely uttering a word to him that wasn't work related. He left her alone, knowing that she would eventually have to let it go and return to her old self. When that old self did return, she was warm and funny like she had always been.

She managed to get past the bonfire incident, even going out with one or two guys afterward. But it hadn't lasted long. In lonely moments the kiss haunted her, spinning her further into the depression that had started after her breakup with John. She found her solace in food and cigarettes, which held each other in check and kept her weight stable for the time being. It seemed to be the only thing going right in her life.

She was more surprised than anyone when Graham had asked her to be his roommate. His idea came the day after she and Helen had decided to do the same thing, so rather than have to decide between the two of them, Mattie came up with the idea of the three of them moving in together – and she was even more shocked when they both agreed. Helen and Graham had only met once after their initial meeting, when he gave her a ride to the cabin. Mattie worried about how they would get along sharing the same apartment, but only for the first couple of weeks. Graham seemed to have successfully buried his interest in Helen, especially when Kevin Delamont would drive down from Valleyview to stay with them on weekends.

"Leave me alone!"

The laughter-filled cry sounded throughout the apartment, known as *the house* to all who lived there. It prompted Mattie to rush a little faster through the remaining few feet of hallway that separated her and their front door. She had only gone down a couple of floors to retrieve something from her car, and now found that Kevin and Graham were ganging up on Helen about some barb that she had just hurled at them. There were grins all around, immediately spreading to Mattie when she stepped inside. Helen ran toward her, nearly knocking the keys from her hand as she spun Mattie around to use her best friend for a shield. "Thank God you're back!" she giggled, shoving Mattie between them. "They've lost their minds!"

"That's supposed to be news?" Mattie countered, twisting herself out of her friend's grip to step aside and drop her keys on the kitchen counter. "Don't drag me into this."

Graham began slinking toward Helen, his hands forming into claws as he moved in villainous, melodramatic fashion. "You can't get out of this," he warned. "You must pay for your lies."

Mattie squinted, cocking her head and folding her arms over her chest when she questioned, "What did you say about him now?"

Helen began to laugh, once again trying to use her friend for a shield. At that moment Graham lunged for the pair, giving Mattie a good-natured grab as he went after Helen. Mattie burst out laughing. Helen wasn't able to provide Mattie with an answer when laughter completely took her over, so she grabbed her by the wrist and dragged her down the hallway and into her bedroom. There they could regroup, and barricade themselves against the enemy that was sure to follow. Each armed themselves with a giant pillow and took aim.

When the men appeared in the doorway a few seconds later, the two had horsing around on their mind. Their weapon – tickling. Each grabbed at the woman that was closest to him. Graham managed to control only one of Helen's wrists in his attack, and actually spent most of his energy trying to get past her free hand and at her sides. Kevin had more luck – he was able to force both of Mattie's wrists into the strong grip of his right hand. As she tried to break free from his grip, she soon realized that he was holding onto her tighter than was necessary. Her immediate instinct was to sink to the ground, hoping that it would give him the idea that he was getting too rough. He went down with her to retain his hold, and before anyone knew it he was straddled across her hips, her right leg painfully pinned underneath her. "Get off!" she warned, trying to push him back.

He was so intent on winning this small battle that he didn't hear her. But tickling had turned into painful poking and scratching that managed to get at the skin underneath her loose shirt. The lack of laughter had drawn Graham and Helen's attention. Mattie's face was turning red, a combination of fear and the lack of air in her lungs. She did, however, manage to draw a deep enough breath to shout at him, "Get the fuck off me!"

"Kevin!" Helen hollered, her hands planting themselves on her hips.

Kevin had finally rolled off of his victim just as Graham jumped to her aid, not allowing Helen's fiancé to say anything as he subtly forced his way in between them. "You alright?" he asked, extending his hand to help Mattie to her feet.

She nodded, shaken but otherwise okay. With his hand on her back, Graham steered her out of the room to guide her away from the looming argument that was about to explode between Helen and Kevin. He sat her down on the couch, then tried to wrap an arm around her shoulders as he sat down beside her. But the second he touched her she jumped back up, grabbing her smokes and her keys before tearing out of the apartment.

Chapter 15

"Is that the last of it?"

Sasha looked up as she kicked the door shut behind her, handing the box full of books to Mark. "That's it," she confirmed, knocking the dust from her clothes and slipping off her shoes. When she followed him into the living room, she found him clearing space on some shelves.

"I hope here is okay," he told her as he loaded one arm with volumes.

"It's fine," she assured, taking some of the weight from him and carrying it into the den.

Together they placed the books in their new home. When they were done, Mark pulled Sasha up against him by the waist and whispered, "Welcome home," just before he kissed her.

Chapter 16

"What the hell do I do now?"

Mattie and Graham were both parked on the beat-up couch on their balcony later that night, feet perched on the railing as they sat in the warm evening air. He had allowed her to sit down next to him and rest her head on his shoulder as she vented, but made no move to try to comfort her again. "She'll think that I'm overreacting." She looked to her best friend. "Do you think I'm overreacting?"

"No."

"So what am I gonna do?" She ran her fingers through her hair and blew a rush of air out between her teeth. "I don't even want to be in the same room with him, never mind be the maid of honor at their wedding."

Through the opened patio window they could hear keys turning over in the lock. "Here she comes," Graham warned, pulling himself up and over the left arm of the couch to reach for his cigarettes.

Helen stepped out onto the balcony just as Mattie got up onto her feet. As they passed each other she said to both her roommates, "I'm going to take a bath."

Helen watched her leave, then turned back to Graham. "What's with her?"

Graham shrugged, just like he always did, and blew out a few smoke rings. "Nothing. She's just tired."

"Oh." She leaned back against the railing, her gaze still inside along with her thoughts. The conclusion wasn't hard for her to reach. "She's mad at Kevin, isn't she?"

"Yeah."

"I'll get him to give her a call."

"Not a good idea."

She looked at him. "Why not?"

He took another pull from the cigarette, taking his time to answer her. Finally he said, "Because then she'll just get mad at you."

"Yeah, I guess you're right," she nodded, a small shiver running down her back. If there was one thing Helen had ever been sure of, it was to stay on Mattie's good side. "I'll see you later." She headed inside, leaving Graham to his own thoughts.

Chapter 17

Months passed for the roommates without any further incidents, and things eventually returned to normal. Mattie kept a wary distance from Kevin now when he visited, trying not to be too obvious in her contempt for him. Most of her time these days was dedicated to self-exploration, something that she had been avoiding ever since her breakup with John. She discovered that her love of song and performing was something more than the nights she and John had spent at karaoke with his friends. With the assistance of the self-help books that she read, she had decided that it was something that she wanted to pursue.

Helen surrounded herself with her plans for her wedding, which she and Kevin decided would be held at her grandmother's farm at the end of May. Her father had been suddenly transferred to Nebraska, so Helen started to rely heavily on Mattie for planning assistance when her mother and sister became too involved with moving. To add to the pressure she felt, Kevin had not had any luck finding a job in Edmonton, so instead he resided with his parents back in Valleyview, six hours away. They made an agreement; until such time as he did find a job he would stay up north, even if it was after they were married. But he would drive down every weekend to be with her, just as he had been doing for the last year. So they started to browse for apartments on the south side of the city, where she could be close to work.

Graham, on the other hand, seemed to be swinging into a deep depression of his own, finding fault with everything in his life. He was slipping into mid-life crisis no matter what he did which, according to Mattie, he was rocketing toward far before his time. Even he realized that he was developing into a champion cynic. So he sat at his computer, smoked his cigarettes, and merely waited for the moods to pass.

Living together sometimes made for a tense situation between Graham and Mattie. Depending on his mood or her anxiety level, Helen either found herself in the middle of a war zone or a mutual admiration society. On good days, she would come home to find the two cuddled together on the couch, or Graham brushing out Mattie's shoulder-length hair. On bad days, especially once Mattie had started to try and quit smoking, Helen would usually just hole up in her room and read to stay out of the line of fire.

On one of their private, 'girls only' days, Helen had remarked that one day Graham was suddenly going to come to his senses and realize that he was in love with Mattie. When her friend demanded an explanation for this theory, Helen pointed out that when Graham held her, he would always gaze down at the unsuspecting young woman with a sense of adoration.

The comment merely added to list of instances that Mattie kept arranged in her mind, of all the times that she and Graham behaved more closely than, and were perceived to be, more than friends. There were many instances of him seeking her out to kiss her, or to stretch out across the couch and rest his head in her lap as they all sat around watching TV. The night before Les and Jennifer's wedding, as Helen's steady hand was painting Mattie's fingernails, he came up behind Mattie and tugged on her ponytail in order to steal a kiss before bed. To anybody else, it would have resulted in high anxiety. To Mattie, it was just the way they were.

Another Friday night brought yet another visit from Kevin, and after dinner he joined the three roommates for an exciting night of television and drinks. Mattie was in a particularly foul mood that evening, having found out during her annual physical earlier that day that smoking cessation had earned her another twenty pounds. So when an ad came on for the local workout guru's daily exercise show, she lunged for the remote control that seemed to always be perched on Graham's thigh.

"What the hell…!" he squawked, instinctively snatching it before she could get it.

"Turn the channel!" she ordered as she made another grab for the remote.

Now Graham held the remote purposely out of her reach. "What for?"

"I hate that fucking woman!" she spat at him, pointing to the leggy blonde stepping her way to health on the screen.

Without thinking Graham shot back, "Only because you're never going to look like her!"

Mattie froze cold, fixing him with the coldest glare imaginable. "Fuck you!" she cursed as she clambered to her feet. Then, as she usually did, she picked up her keys and started to flee rather than confront him.

"What did I do now?" he called out after her as he turned to follow.

Helen was stunned, but she waited until Mattie slammed the door shut behind her. "What the hell is wrong with you?" she yelled at him, untangling herself from Kevin's arms and jumping to her feet.

"What?"

Graham looked completely honest in his ignorance, which infuriated Helen even further. "You just told her that she's always going to be fat no matter what she does!"

He started to light a cigarette as he dismissed, "No I didn't."

Incensed, Helen stormed over and ripped the cigarette out of his mouth before he could put a flame to it. "Why do you have to be such an asshole?" she shouted, hurling the tobacco across the room. "Are you scared of her or something?"

"Hey! That's my last one!"

Helen followed him as he scrambled to retrieve his smoke. "You *are* afraid of her!"

"No I'm not!"

"You are!" she continued. "You're afraid that if she gets skinny, she won't want to be around you anymore!"

"I don't give a fuck what she wants!" Graham roared back at her. "I was just telling the truth!"

Helen gasped at him, stunned silent by his response. Eventually she quietly said, "One day you're going to figure out that you don't have to hurt her before she can hurt you." With that, she headed out the front door. "Matt!"

Graham stood there for a while, staring at the closed door. Mattie's sensibilities were really beginning to grate on him, and what had started as a perfectly fine evening had now ended up being full of tension and hurt feelings. Graham still didn't think he'd said anything wrong – and he was especially unimpressed with Helen's unnecessary defense.

Kevin squirmed uncomfortably from his place in the corner. Mattie was getting on his nerves as well, but mostly because she had become a point of contention between him and Helen. His fiancée had read him the riot act after the tickling incident, and it had turned into an ugly fight between them. As they got closer to their wedding, he realized that Helen was more of a free spirit than he initially thought. And it bothered him.

He eventually asked Graham, "Wanna go get a beer?"

"Sure." Graham opened his hand, which now held the cigarette that he had unconsciously crushed. He cursed as he got his coat, now forced to make a smoke run rather than just heading straight to the bar. The girls were nowhere to be found when they left, which already made it easier for him to begin forgetting the whole thing.

Mattie was usually the last one to leave in the mornings, even when she was on time for work. With her bedroom sandwiched between Helen's and the living room, she would have to be extremely quiet as she got ready on the rare mornings that Helen didn't start work until noon. But when she knew that Helen was already gone, Mattie would take the opportunity to warm up her voice by singing along with the radio. It was nothing new – she had been doing it for years. But now that she was pursuing a singing career, it was more than idle song. It was a rehearsal session.

She had barely spoken two words to Graham since their blow-up on Friday night, and he had wisely kept his distance from her. She was still seething with anger over what he had said, and drowning with self-doubt because she secretly believed that he was right. It didn't seem to matter what she did lately, everything was going wrong. The politics at work were driving her crazy, and she was making so little that she couldn't put together enough money to cut a demo. But the icing on the cake had been the weight gain, caused by the healthy intention of quitting smoking. She was trying everything to get ahead, and was falling behind instead. But at least she had Helen there to help her through all of it. Her best friend was a never-ending source of support, mental and otherwise. She sometimes thought that Helen believed in her talents more than she did.

Helen had left for work at six that morning, so Mattie was taking full advantage of it and sang away as she started getting dressed. She was doing up the last of the buttons on her blouse when the song she had been hoping to hear came on the radio, a little tinny through the old digital alarm clock. It was a song heavy in social connotations, and Mattie admired the determination of the songwriter to push a touchy subject even further into the open with it. She stood there long after she was dressed in order to finish the song, closing her eyes and visualizing being in a spotlight on a darkened stage. The feeling of contentment lingered for a few moments after the song was done, before she shook it away and headed across the hall to finish fixing her hair in the bathroom.

A short, frightened yelp was ripped from her when she saw someone out of the corner of her eye. Graham was standing at the end of the hallway, leaning against the corner that formed where the hallway and living room met, his soft brown eyes gazing directly at her. His posture did not change when she came out of the room, his expression one of pure captivation. He had been listening to her sing, and was so mesmerized that he hadn't noticed her entrance into the hall.

Her heart was pounding, her pulse thudding loudly in her ears. "Jesus!" she gasped, her hand instinctively covering her chest as she heaved a breath. "Don't do that!"

It took a moment more for him to break himself out of his haze. For once he didn't adopt his usual, brash attitude when he quietly apologized, "Sorry. I didn't mean to scare you."

She stared back at him, so involved in the adrenaline running through her body that she really didn't notice his pensive mood until he left. It replayed in her head as she fussed with her hair in the bathroom mirror. In retrospect, she realized that he had been listening intently to her when she surprised him, enough so that it took him a moment or two to realize what had happened. Considering that she was convinced he really never listened to anything she said anyway, she wondered just what this meant for their relationship. The softness of his expression was different than anything she had ever seen in him before.

She had entranced him.

Chapter 18

Les came home from school around seven-thirty, exhausted by the three hour lab that ended his Tuesdays. He heard his wife call a greeting to him, and once his shoes were off he found her in the center of the couch, surrounded by books. "Hi," he said, leaning down to kiss her. Then he took a moment to examine the mayhem around her. "Whatcha doin'?" he asked in his best imitation of a four-year-old.

"Reading," she said flatly, just to see what kind of response she would get.

He shrugged. "Okay."

She caught the back pocket on his jeans before he could leave and pulled him down next to her. "Most of the university calendars I sent away for arrived today." Jennifer gathered up a few and handed them to her husband.

He leafed through the variety – University of Calgary, Mount Royal, University of Toronto…"Med school, huh?" he mused aloud, flipping through some pages.

"Yep."

Les looked up at her, and he couldn't help but smile at her enthusiasm. If she was going to do something, she threw her whole self into it. As he turned back to his reading, a brightly colored book on the coffee table caught his attention. "Dalhousie?" he said, reaching forward to pick it up.

She nodded. "I wasn't going to send for it."

"So how come you did?"

"Mattie convinced me," she said with a laugh. "But I don't know if I'll apply."

Les fixed his clear blue eyes on her as he questioned, "Why not?"

"Well it's med school," she pointed out, her own eyes meeting his. "Besides, it's in Halifax."

"So what?" Jennifer's shoulders dropped, and her head cocked to the right – her classic look of surprise when he said something she didn't expect. She had fully expected him to agree with her; after all, Halifax was on the east coast. Their families were here, their friends were here – their lives were here. "It's not going to hurt to apply," he pointed out, "and if you do get accepted, we'll worry about it then."

She thought about it for a bit, then half-grinned in resignation. "You're as bad as Mattie."

Les returned her smile, relieved that she was going to at least consider it. "Well then I'm in good company," he told her as he kissed the top of her head. "She's a very wise woman."

Chapter 19

"We're never going to get there on time!"

Mattie's knuckles were white around the steering wheel of her two-seat Sprint convertible, her knee tense from holding the accelerator down to the floor. She scanned erratically for cops as they flew down the highway, concentrating more on making sure that they got there in one piece. After taking a corner on two wheels early into the trip, she made sure to be a little more careful with each turn. They were condensing an hour's drive into thirty minutes, and she cursed the fact that her little car topped out at only a hundred and forty.

In the passenger seat beside her, Helen was sitting in a somewhat altered lotus position, her hands clutching two little Animaniacs figures that Mattie had given her the year before and chanting, "Llama, llama, llama..." to keep herself calm. At Mattie's last outburst she told her, "We're going to get there. Just take it easy." Her eyes opened when she felt the car slow to turn off the highway.

A continuous cloud of dust flew up into the air as they sped down the gravel road, washed-out bits rattling their teeth as they flew over it. Finally the farmyard came into sight, and Mattie could see that it was already filled with wedding guests, their vehicles and tents for some to stay overnight. She let out a sigh of relief as she looked at the clock in the dashboard – it was five minutes to one.

Unlike Mattie, Helen started to suddenly get nervous. Everybody was there already, and yet her parents were still behind them and were making stops to pick up shoes for her sister and a suit for her father. "Shit, we're late!" she cursed as she started gathering her things up.

The guests for Kevin and Helen's wedding had assembled all around the central area that made up the farmyard. There were no chairs put out for them, so they all gathered in small clutches to chat as they waited for the ceremony to start. All the groomsmen were dressed in their tuxedos and were ready to go. But there was no sign of the bride, her attendants, or her immediate family.

Graham, who had been banished from Kevin's sight as long as there was a cigarette in his mouth, was wandering down the edge of the lane when he heard a car coming down the road. As the emcee he was dressed in the same ensemble as the groom, but served as a go-between to keep everybody apprised of what was going on. In a few seconds, Mattie's small blue convertible turned the corner, yet again on two wheels, and raced down to park beside the house. It slid to a halt, spitting rocks across Graham's patent shoes and a plume of dust on his tuxedo as he ran up to open the passenger door. "Right on time," he told Helen, sarcasm at the ready. Helen growled something incomprehensible at him as she got out, the calm woman from the highway long gone.

Mattie looked over to see that Kevin's best man had covered the groom's eyes, then steered Helen toward the side door of the house. Jennifer rushed over to join them. "Where are your mom and dad?"

"They should be right behind us," Mattie told her.

Helen added, "They still had to stop and pick stuff up." She reached the side door first, but when she tried to open it, discovered that it was locked. "Fuck!" she cursed under her breath. "Fuck, fuck, fuck, fuck!"

"Hang on a second!" Graham called back as he headed for the corner of the house. "I'll open it."

Mattie couldn't help but giggle as she told Jennifer, "You know, she was perfectly fine until we hit the driveway."

"Well the way that you were driving, one of us had to be," the bride shot back, nervously chewing at her nail and wishing that Graham would get his ass in gear.

Her maid of honor feigned offence. "I got you here, didn't I?"

Helen started pacing within a small square. "Yeah. And almost rolled the car in the process."

Mattie and Jennifer exchanged bemused glances. "We can go back and do it again if you like," she taunted.

The door opened to reveal Helen's grandmother, their host for the day. "Come on," she told them, extending her hand to her granddaughter. "Let's get you dressed."

On the lawn behind the house, Kevin was starting to wear a groove in the grass beside the sidewalk. Everyone's eyes turned again to the driveway when a large black sedan pulled up. Helen's parents and sister all jumped out and headed for the side entrance, where Helen's grandmother was still waiting for them. Shaking his head in disgust, Kevin muttered, "You'd think that they could at least be on time for their own daughter's wedding."

In the bedroom on the west side of the house, Mattie and Jennifer were busy trying to get Helen in order. Helen's mother, sister and grandmother were also crammed into the tiny room, trying to get themselves together. It left very little room for movement, and all kinds of opportunity for tempers to flare. Helen's younger sister Erin was the first to be dressed, demonstrating the fact when she asked, "Is everybody ready?"

The two siblings had been at each other all morning at the hair salon, so their mother could sense another fight coming on. "Go tell them we'll be out in two minutes."

Erin left, which gave her grandmother a little room to maneuver when she stepped over to kiss the bride before she left. Jennifer finished with the buckle on Helen's shoe, then stood up and took her friend's hand. "Remember to have fun," she advised.

Helen's head was jerked back as her mother fussed with the combs that would hold her veil into place. "I'll try," she told Jennifer, absently taking her hand away to try and keep her hair from being ripped out.

Mattie told Helen, "I'll see you down in front," then followed Jennifer out into the kitchen.

Left alone for the moment, mother and daughter took a good look at one another. "I'm sorry we're so rushed," her mother said as she fussed with the curls that framed her daughter's face.

Helen looked at her mother. She had been responsible for booking the hair appointments in a shop over an hour away from the wedding site, and for not booking the appointments early enough that morning. The wedding started at one o'clock, and between the short-staffed shop, the tense atmosphere between the sisters and her father only arriving at 11:30 that morning from the States, Helen had already been frazzled by the time Mattie floored her tiny Sprint to get them there in time. But for the first time since their light speed trip from the hair shop, Helen took a second to breathe. "It's okay. I'm just glad you're here."

The wedding was running so late that the justice of the peace was threatening to leave in order to meet his own schedule that day. Kevin sent Graham to find out what was taking so long, and when he blew in through the door he nearly ran headlong into Mattie on the landing. Her sudden stop was too quick for Jennifer, who in a moment of distraction hit her from behind. This jarred the bouquet from Mattie's hands, which Graham's quick reaction caught before they could hit the floor. "And you say I never bring you flowers," he quipped, handing them back to her.

"You don't," she flatly reminded him as she took the bouquet back. "We're just about ready here."

"Right." He started to leave, but turned back and grabbed her hand to pull her close. "You look great," he whispered into her ear. Then he left just as quickly.

Jennifer still stood behind Mattie, her eyes wide from witnessing the exchange. "He is *so* in love with you," she murmured.

Mattie whirled around. "No, he's not."

Her friend shook her head. "I'm telling you, it's true."

"You're out of your mind."

Before Jennifer could pursue the matter further, Helen appeared at the top of the stairs and was blinded by the sunlight that flashed off the still-closing screen door. Once she could see again, she rolled her eyes and muttered, "I should have worn my sunglasses."

"How are you doing?" Mattie checked.

"I'm nervous."

"You got your Kleenex?"

"Right here." Helen turned her bouquet to the side to show her friend the wad of tissues that had been wrapped around the plastic handle. Then she extended a hand to Mattie so that she could be helped down the couple of steps to the door.

In front of them, Erin had her nose pressed to the door to watch the people outside. Down at the archway, the justice of the peace had joined Kevin and Brad, and on seeing the young girl at the door motioned for her to start the procession. Erin looked back to everyone for their approval, then carefully went outside.

For a split second, Mattie turned to her best friend. "Here goes nothin'."

Helen nodded. "Wild women do." With their free hands, the pair hit their fists on top of one another, and then Mattie led the way out the door.

Helen's grandfather was seated at his small keyboard near the archway, and he started to sing a generic love song as the girls started walking down the sidewalk from the house. Mattie had to bite her tongue to keep from laughing at his horribly off-key warbling. She looked over to Graham, who knew exactly what she was thinking and gave her an amused little shrug. It was enough to keep her happy and from concentrating on her negative feelings while Helen, as Mattie had put it to Graham the night before, sealed her impending fate.

Chapter 20

Dear El,

Hope the honeymoon is going well. How's Florida?

I found a new place on the south side – not too far away from yours, actually. It's a great place that overlooks the river valley and freeway – I just wish they would fix the lock on the door downstairs.

Helen's wedding had marked the end of the roommate phase of Mattie's life. She and Graham were cycling through their relationship as usual, and in the aftermath of the wedding, animosity between Graham and Mattie was at an all-time high. She had gotten quite angry with him when he told her that he didn't want to continue living with her, and he knew why she was so mad – she had been working on the assumption that the two of them would just find their own place together after Helen left. But her angry phases really didn't bother him anymore.

He had been able to make arrangements to move into his new place during the last two days of the month, while she wouldn't have access to hers until the first. So he left a disaster in his wake, and an oblivious disregard for any feelings that he may have been treading on when he left.

Mattie had found herself a place on the south side of the city, only a few blocks away from both Jennifer and Helen. On the fifth floor of a six-storey tower, it overlooked the in-city ski hill that was just on the other side of the freeway. It was expensive, and the largest floor plan in the building, but she felt that it was worth it. Being a country girl, she had never been comfortable with other people being able to look into her windows on a regular basis. But as the building manager had said to her when she signed the lease agreement, "The only way that someone can spy on you is to stand at the top of the ski hill with binoculars."

She did her best to make light of the fact that she was now going to be living completely on her own, finding every advantage that she could in it. The large space allowed her to finally have her piano, which was an heirloom purchased by her grandparents fifty years earlier. Another was the fact that she could have a cat, which was also something that she missed from her childhood. She eventually chose a small black and white kitten and called him Max. Like any kitten, he had boundless energy and curiosity to explore his new surroundings.

After she had unpacked all her things, it took a great deal of time for Mattie to carry all of the garbage and collapsed boxes to the chute down the hall. She propped the door open with a book to make the job easier, so Max took frequent advantage of the freedom and would trot out behind her to check things out. She caught him every time as she came back, gleefully chasing him back inside by stomping her feet. So when she made her last trip down the hall, it was no surprise that he followed her. But this time, the door across the hall opened. Seeing it as another avenue of exploration, Max bolted into the stranger's kitchen. The man was quick, but almost not enough as he stumbled after the little furball. Once the kitten was in his possession, he scratched it underneath the chin and stepped out into the hallway.

For a moment there was no one, and then he heard soft singing as she stepped back into the hallway. He took a moment to check her out before she could catch him at it. Hers was a simple beauty, not like the anorexic, weight-obsessed girls he usually was attracted to. But to him, from the little bit that he had heard, the most remarkable thing about her was her voice. As soon as she saw the kitten in his hands, a sheepish grin spread across her face. "I think this belongs to you," he said, handing it back to her as soon as she was within reach.

"You little bugger!" she scolded Max as she took him.

The man laughed. "Little nothing. He just about knocked my guitar off its stand."

She looked up from the cat, her curiosity piqued. "You're a musician?"

"Yeah," he nodded. "I'm Zack, by the way."

She shook the hand he offered. "Mattie."

"I hope I won't keep you awake with my playing. I tend to go pretty late."

"Well, if you do, I'll just start banging on the piano. Then they'll kick both of us out."

He laughed again, then a glance at his watch reminded him that he had been on his way out. "I've gotta run," he announced, pulling the door shut behind him. "I'll see you later."

"You bet," she replied, heading for her own door.

The elevator was only a few feet away, and as he waited for the heavy door to slide open, he suggested, "I'd love to hear you sing sometime."

Caught, Mattie's cheeks flushed with embarrassment. She had assumed no one had been listening. "I'll think about that," she said as the elevator door slid shut.

Chapter 21

Helen's new apartment was one that was comfortably cluttered, a threadbare old couch and a couple of lounging chairs crammed into its narrow living room. She lived here alone most of the time, much more than she had anticipated after she and Kevin got married. He would drive down on Friday nights after he was finished work, stay the weekend, then leave late Sunday afternoon to make the drive back to Valleyview. To combat her loneliness, Helen had made arrangements with her best friend for a weekly visit on Sunday night to watch their favorite serial romance – the same one that they had started watching along with Graham the year before. It gave them the chance to get together and bash or pine over men, depending on Mattie's mood that day.

The last Sunday before Christmas was no exception, and the indulgence of choice was miniature brownies that Jennifer had baked for them, each topped with a large chocolate rosette. Helen crumpled the muffin paper in her fingertips, then tossed it onto the growing pile on the coffee table. Part of the pile was pushed out of the way when Mattie threw her feet up onto it and settled back into the worn brown fabric of the couch. "Do you think I'll ever get married?" she mused suddenly.

"Without a doubt." Unable to get comfortable, Helen got up and grabbed her body pillow to stretch out on the floor.

Mattie looked at her friend as she maneuvered herself into a new position, careful not to put too much pressure on

her occupied abdomen. "Do you like being married?" she
asked her.

For a moment, Mrs. Delamont had to think about her
answer – no one had ever asked her what she thought about
it. "Yeah, I do," she finally said, unable to hide the hesitation
in her answer. "It isn't what I expected…but I do."

Mattie considered calling Helen on her obvious
misgivings, but decided against it. Her mistrust of Kevin had
only grown in the months since their wedding, but she had to
keep reminding herself that her feelings about Kevin
Delamont didn't matter. Helen would most likely take
Mattie's best intentions the wrong way if she said anything
and disappear out of her life forever. So she buried her
feelings, holding on tightly to the friend who she realized
meant more to her than any other person. "Would it be
wrong," she said, suddenly changing the subject, "if I said
that all I wanted right now was pure, animal sex?"

"Absolutely not." Helen found that she was still
uncomfortable, and she adjusted her position again as she
suggested, "What about that guy that lives across the hall
from you? You said he was pretty cute."

"Zack?" Mattie thought back to the night before, which
she had spent watching her neighbor play onstage in one of
the local bars. She nodded and confirmed, "He is. But I don't
feel anything for him. He's just fun to hang around with."

"Well, there's something to be said for that too," Helen
said with a shrug.

The pair lapsed into silence, enraptured by a scene on
the television. When it switched to a commercial, Helen
slowly pulled herself up and headed for the bathroom,
leaving Mattie alone. Mattie never pried or nosed around her
friend's place – she had never felt the need to. But that night,
piled on the corner of the coffee table next to her feet, were a
bunch of multicolored pamphlets. Curiosity got the better of
her, and she grunted with effort as she reached forward to
grab them. They were typical information packages on

childbirth and pre-natal care, all the things that doctors like to give their obstetrics patients to read.

Helen came back around the corner and saw her friend looking at one of the pamphlets. Mattie looked up when she came back into the living room, and she reached out to touch Helen. "God, you are getting so big."

Helen grinned, instinctively running her hand over her belly. "I had my first appointment with the obstetrician on Friday," she told her guest, pointing to the paper in Mattie's hand.

"How did it go?"

"Pretty good. But he says that I have to register for my pre-natal classes now. Apparently they fill up pretty fast."

"So...when's Kevin moving down here?" Mattie asked, fully aware that she was not going to like the answer.

Helen sat down on the couch beside her. "We don't know yet. He hasn't been able to find a job here."

Mattie dropped the pamphlet back down on the table. "Still nothing?"

"No." Unbelievably, Helen was still unaware of Mattie's impression of the whole situation, so she felt no guilt in telling her. "But he makes more doing construction in Valleyview than I do at the shop. So it all kind of works out in the end."

"Yeah," the other grumbled. "But what good is a husband when he lives half a province away?"

"Not much." They became engrossed in the storyline again, but Helen was distracted by nerves. "Listen...I want to ask you something."

"What's that?" her friend asked automatically, still concentrating on the television.

Figuring that there was no reason to beat about the issue, the expectant mother said, "Will you go to my pre-natal classes with me? I want you to be my coach."

There was a slow, almost exaggerated progression through Mattie's emotions. First she stopped chewing her brownie, then widened eyes slowly made their way across the room to land on the woman that sat beside her. And in a few seconds, those eyes shimmered with the tears that were welling up in them. "Really?"

Helen nodded. "I don't know when Kevin will be moving down here, and the classes are on Tuesdays and Thursdays, so he won't be able to drive down. Besides, when I go into labor, I'll need somebody here now, and not have to wait for hours for Kevin to get here." She smiled nervously. "Will you do it?"

Mattie grinned with glee. "Of course I'll do it!" The pair hugged each other tightly, and over Helen's shoulder Mattie whispered, "I'm so honored that you asked me."

"I wouldn't have asked anyone else."

But before Mattie could even get to the first childbirth class, Helen announced that she was picking up and moving to Valleyview to join her husband. Mattie was immediately enraged, and utterly inconsolable. The man that she hated more than any in the world was not only taking over her friend's life and shutting her off from the remaining family she had in the area, but he was also taking away an experience that Mattie was looking forward to – it was as close to being a mother herself as she ever thought she could get. She always remembered how her parents' friends had been treated as her aunts and uncles and, being a single child, she couldn't wait for the opportunity to have her own niece or nephew to dote on.

When Helen first told her, Mattie tried her best to give the impression of her approval. She couldn't tell whether her friend was convinced, but she really didn't care. The more she thought about the situation, the more she hated it. Hate turned to anger, and anger into helplessness and frustration. And despite her promise to come help them load the truck on the final day, Mattie was so distraught that she couldn't bring herself to do it.

Helen paced up and down the sidewalk in front of the apartment building, basically staying out of her husband's way as he and his best friend loaded the last of the boxes into the truck. Her impatience was starting to get the better of her, and she couldn't help but scowl as she checked the street in each direction. There was still no sign of the little blue car.

When the last box was loaded and the keys returned to the building manager, Kevin stopped and watched his wife for a moment. She was obviously angry, but he wasn't quite sure what about. When she paced back in his direction he said, "What's the matter?"

"Mattie was supposed to be here," she said tersely, continuing to move right past him.

"Maybe she forgot," he offered, trying his best to sound sincere. "She can be pretty absent-minded."

"Not like this." She checked her watch and then the street again.

Kevin walked over and put his arm around Helen's shoulders. "Don't worry about it. I bet she just forgot," he assured her. "Call her when we get home."

"I guess so." She let him lead her to the passenger door of the rental truck, then climbed inside. In the time that she waited for him to get to the driver's seat, she continued to watch for Mattie's car. But as they pulled out to head north, her worst fear had been confirmed.

Her best friend had not come to say goodbye.

Chapter 22

Tender kisses over her eyes started to pull Sasha from her realm of dreams. She sighed, enjoying the sensations of floating between sleep and pleasurable reality. The kisses moved across her body, working their way down her arms and legs and up the center of her torso before finally reaching her lips. The searing contact there brought her fully alert, her eyes popping open just as Mark pulled away from her. He smiled. "I was beginning to wonder if you were ever going to wake up."

She smiled slightly, lifting her hand and clumsily cupping his cheek. "Is there something I can do for you?" she asked, her voice thick with sleep.

He shifted his weight so that he was partially laying on top of her, but still keeping most of his body on the mattress. When he did, she could feel his intentions pressing against her hip. In between kisses he said, "I was wondering if you might be open for business."

Her smile widened, excited at the prospect of a surprise encounter in the dead of night. It had been a while. Running her other hand up over her mate's chest, she encircled his neck and pulled him close. "I suppose I could start a little early today." Her eyes locked with his, and she added, "For a price."

Paying her price meant a long session ahead, one that Mark was quite willing to embark on. He kissed her with a grin, then slowly worked his way down to nuzzle her breast. A free hand worked at her right while he continued to taste the other, until the fingers in his hair directed him to switch sides. Sasha's head was thrown back hard into the pillow, eyes squeezed shut as she felt each flick of his tongue on her skin. Those eyes relaxed, then finally opened when she realized that his ministrations had stopped. He was carefully rubbing across a small section on her left breast. "What?"

He frowned, squinting as he tried to get a better look in the limited light. "This." His fingertips continued to explore as they put pressure down on her flesh. Her frown matched his as she reached down to examine what had intrigued him. She knew what it was the second she touched it. He looked at her, reaching the same conclusion at the same time. "Oh Christ..." he murmured.

She bolted upright, throwing him back toward the foot of the bed. When he reached for her she sharply bit at him, "No!" And then Mark could only watch in silence as she left the room.

After a brief interlude of not seeing each other, Mattie and Graham finally managed to get organized enough to be able to spend an evening together. They had gone out for dinner at their favorite restaurant, then traveled back to his apartment to play with the piano. He was extremely talkative – she was a little on the quiet side. They both shed their coats and shoes and then went into the living room.

"So if they hire me at head office, I could get my work visa and go to California," he told her, lifting the lid to reveal the black and white keys.

"So what's stopping you from applying?" she asked from the kitchen, where she was getting a glass of water.

Graham's absent plunking on the keys underscored the next bit of their conversation. "I don't speak French," he said matter-of-factly.

"So?"

"People in our California office think that everyone in Canada speaks French. And more to the point, that no one in Quebec wants to speak English."

She laughed as she came back into the living room with her glass. "So apply anyway. What can it hurt?"

He started to play the beginning of the song that they had been working on together. "You know, if I got the job in Sacramento," he told her, "I'd marry you so you could get your green card."

"Really?" She set the glass down on the desk behind him, playfully rubbing his earlobe as she whispered, "That is the most half-assed proposal I've ever heard."

A little smile crossed his lips, but then he decided to change the subject. "I've been working on the song," he told her as he went back to the beginning. "I think I fixed that problem with the sixteenth bar." He started to play their new arrangement.

Mattie allowed her eyes to slide closed, and she hummed softly until she started to sing. Her voice filled his small apartment, resonating off the pale walls that formed the living room. The smoothness of the voice faltered when she felt a growing discomfort quickly spreading across her lower back. Her concentration slipped, and her brow furrowed as she tried to ignore it. She continued to sing with a burst of strength that only lasted for a phrase before the discomfort turned into pain that spread around to the front of her body and crawled up underneath her ribcage. Her knuckles quickly turned white when she grabbed the back of the office chair. Mattie tried to carry on, but only got a few more words out before the pain made breathing difficult.

Graham continued playing, engrossed in his music and not necessarily depending on Mattie's voice. It wasn't unusual for her to drop off when she had difficulty with a few notes, or if she reached a section she was unfamiliar with. He let the last pair of chords linger before slowly lifting them off the keys and flipping back to the first sheet of music. "So what do you think?"

Mattie was still trying to get a handle on what was happening to her, and through clenched teeth she growled, "Hang on a minute." She sat on the corner of the desk, doubling over as she tried to appease whatever had gotten hold of her. Graham didn't even look back over his shoulder, but merely went back to the keys again.

It passed within a few minutes and never appeared again, but it made Mattie realize just how unobservant he could be. She cried when she returned home that night, knowing that he was not as in tune with her as she thought she was with him. And yet again she lapsed further into depression, wondering why she had invested so much time in a man who didn't seem to even know that she loved him.

Chapter 23

Victoria Day was a blessing for Mattie. After attending a wedding on Saturday and then visiting her parents on Sunday, it was a wonderful thing to be able to sleep late one more day. She staggered out of her bedroom around nine, and immediately planted herself down on the couch to watch American morning talk shows.

The phone rang at ten. Still not fully awake, it was an uneasy journey to get to the phone that hung on the wall before the answering machine could pick it up. She lifted the receiver and then promptly dropped it through clumsy fingers, somehow catching it again with a three-part acrobatic feat before it hit the carpet. "Hello?" she rasped, vocal skills at this time of day not amongst her most refined talents.

"Did I wake you up?" Jennifer asked, busily gathering papers off of her dining room table.

"No." Mattie blindly headed back toward the living room, too tired to notice that Max was at her feet and desperately trying to get her attention so he could be let out onto the balcony. The large tomcat was enough to facilitate an elaborate dance before his human was able to regain her balance. He howled a loud protest to being stepped on, and in return she scolded, "Well move, for Christ's sake!"

Jennifer stood upright for a second, frowning at what she heard. "What's the matter?"

"My cat's trying to kill me," Mattie told her, finally flopping back down into her place on the couch.

Jennifer pushed her head a little tighter against her left shoulder, securing the phone as she carried a pile of term papers to the couch so she could continue her grading from the night before. Her excitement at seeing their friend again was bubbling inside her, and especially the chance to see her newborn son Paul. "I can't wait to see Helen's baby," she told Mattie. "Have you heard from her yet?"

Mattie pulled her feet up underneath the grey comforter that was tossed haphazardly across the couch. "No," she told Jennifer. "But she's supposed to call when they come into town so we can pick a place to meet them."

Jennifer took a small pile of papers into her lap. "Do you think he'll be with her?"

"Undoubtedly," Mattie frowned. "She has to get around somehow." She unconsciously shook her head, still amazed that Helen had never bothered to get a driver's license. There was no reply, and she could hear rustling sounds through the receiver. "What are you doing?"

"Trying to mark term papers for my old professor. But I can't find my pen." A few more seconds of shuffling finally revealed her prize. It had been concealed underneath the magazine that her husband had surreptitiously left open for her to see, showing her the place he thought they should travel to on their upcoming wedding anniversary. She snatched it up off the polished wood surface, a smile of victory on her lips. "Ah hah!"

"You must have found it." Mattie commented absently as she flipped through channels.

"Yeah." She reached for her own remote, tapping the mute button to avoid being distracted. "Did she say what time they were coming into town?"

"No."

Jennifer thought for a moment, then suggested, "Maybe we should call her. Where are they staying?"

"At her grandparents'," Mattie recalled, absently surfing through uninteresting shows. Her fingers rubbed at her left eye, then unconsciously ran through the length of her hair. "But I don't have the number."

At Jennifer's suggestion, they searched for the woman's number in their own respective telephone directories. But there were three numbers under the correct last name, and neither one could remember if they had ever heard what Helen's grandfather's name was. Then Jennifer hit on an idea. Helen's other grandmother, the one that had hosted her wedding, lived just outside a town with less than one thousand people. There could hardly be many listings there for a name like Lewiston. Mattie cut off her conversation with her friend to call this woman, who she hoped would remember her from the summer before.

When the phone was answered, the older woman immediately remembered Helen's maid of honor. Mattie wondered whether or not it was a bad sign. Mrs. Lewiston had been nothing but a cranky old bat from the first time they met, showing a great display of her disapproval when Mattie invited Graham to Helen's wedding shower. But the woman was gracious, supplying her with the telephone number that she required. Mattie reconfirmed the number, and very sweetly thanked Mrs. Lewiston before hanging up to call Mrs. Morrow. After three and a half rings, the line was connected, and a short and precise conversation followed. In less than five minutes Mattie was back on the phone with Jennifer, in a highly irritated state.

Jennifer reached across her papers, careful not to spill any on the floor when she grabbed for the ringing phone on the coffee table. "Hello?"

"Jen, it's me."

The smile returned to her face. "So where are we meeting them?"

"We're not."

The smile instantly faded, her pen dropping onto the carpet with a small thud. "What do you mean we're not?" The frustrated rush of air over the receiver on the other end of the line told her that something was definitely wrong.

"I just talked to her grandmother," her friend recounted, trying to keep her previous conversation straight in her mind so that she could repeat it properly. "I asked her if Helen was around, and she said that they'd gone out. So I asked her when she thought they might be back." A few tears were quickly welling up in her eyes, transferring their hidden rage into a shaking voice. "She said that they probably weren't going to. Kevin said that they were going to stop to get groceries, and then they were heading home."

There was a long, silent pause. Then Jennifer finally said, "I thought that you talked to her on Friday."

"I did," Mattie confirmed. "I did. She wanted to meet Saturday, but we couldn't because of Tammy and Rob's wedding. Then she asked me about yesterday, but that was out because you had to be at the gift opening. But I told her that I had already checked with you, and that any time today would be great. She said that she couldn't wait to see us." The tip of her tongue appeared at the corner of the mouth, catching the tear that had rolled down from her eye.

The other let out a sigh of exasperation. "I can't believe that she didn't call."

Mattie spat, "I can." She realized now that this was just another sign of Kevin's control tactics. When she and Jennifer had visited them just after Paul was born, they spent twelve hours visiting and Kevin never left their sight once. Jennifer had commented in the car how it seemed like he was staying there to keep an eye on things which, despite Mattie's hatred of the man, was something that she had never noticed him doing before.

Her anger was getting the better of her now, her throat growing tight as she spoke. "She loses her head whenever she's with that son of a bitch."

Mattie collapsed into frustrated tears after she got off the phone with Jennifer, but hurriedly cut them short when Graham happened to call. Though she vehemently denied it, he could hear her stuffed nose and occasional tear through the line. For once, he managed to catch onto an emotional outburst that he would normally be oblivious to, so he insisted on taking her out to get her mind off her problems. They took an impromptu coffee trip to Calgary, using the six hours of open road to sing or bullshit, but never to touch on the subject of Helen.

They pulled back up in front of her building at around two in the morning. Mattie was tired, her mind no less settled than when they left town that afternoon. She had to admit that Graham had gone to great pains to try and make her feel better. So after a few parting words, she leaned over to kiss him goodnight.

He hesitated slightly, mentally pulling back for a confused split-second before coming back to the goodbye kiss he was in the middle of. Graham felt her presence in front of him, the waft of her gentle scent around him, and long-dormant desire stirred within him. But he knew those feelings were inappropriate, especially considering that she had suddenly been faced with the fact that she was no longer important in her other best friend's life. And he discovered all of this in less than one line of the song that was currently playing on the radio.

Though exhausted, Mattie felt no desire for sleep. She absently pulled at a cigarette as she watched Graham's departure from her balcony. Once he was gone, she needed something to do. Her clipboard was sitting on her cluttered coffee table, a pile of loose leaf pages stacked neatly under the clip. She made a beeline for it, stopping only long enough to turn on a solitary light and crush out her cigarette before retreating to her usual corner of the couch.

The pen shook in her hand, hovering above the pulp-ridden surface as she thought. She knew what she wanted to say, but was finding it hard to put it into coherent words. After an agonizing period of time, she began.

Dear Helen,

I know that you're not going to like what I have to say, but I've been keeping this locked up inside me for a long time now. For the sake of my own peace of mind, I can't keep it in any longer.

Her eyes lifted from the letter, memories of the shared apartment flooding back. To her surprise, she remembered being home by herself on a Saturday afternoon, two months before the wedding.

Helen was still at work, while Graham and Kevin had gone out to get fitted for tuxedoes. They burst into the room around three o'clock, their enthusiasm damping the peace that Mattie had been enjoying. Her eyes burned with annoyance, then softened as she looked from one to the other and saw the grins on their faces. "Alright, what have you been up to?" she questioned warily, not really sure she wanted to know.

"We got the greatest idea to surprise Helen," Kevin reported, the catalogue from the tux shop still rolled up in his hand.

She folded her arms across her chest. "As Maid of Honor, do I get let in on this surprise?"

They were worse than a pair of five-year-olds. "Yes, but you can't tell," Graham warned.

It was obvious that they were not going to get anywhere until she vowed. "Okay, I promise."

Kevin unrolled the magazine and handed it to her. It was a picture of a group of groomsmen, with their pants around their ankles, displaying cartoon-covered boxer shorts. Mattie burst out laughing, looking up to find both hovering over her. "You're not serious." To answer her,

Graham pulled a pair of black silk boxers out of a shopping bag – ones that prominently displayed Mickey Mouse – and handed them over for her to inspect. Mattie held them at arm's length for a bit, her hands falling into her lap as she shook her head. "You guys are nuts."

Graham leaned down close, millimeters from her face. "Promise you won't tell," he breathed, looking deep into her eyes.

She stared right back at him until she could no longer contain her laughter. "Alright, alright I promise."

"Good." He kissed her, grabbed the boxers from her hands and headed off into his bedroom. Kevin had already disappeared into Helen's room, mercifully leaving Mattie alone. She still was quite wary of him, but had stuck to her promise to keep her mouth shut for Helen's sake.

> *I've sat by and watched as Kevin has slowly taken over your life. He's managed to separate you from your family and your friends and dragged you off to a part of the world where you're surrounded by things familiar only to him. For somebody who promised that he was going to join you where you lived, he never lifted a finger to do it. He just used the coincidence of you getting pregnant to get his way.*
>
> *I'm scared of him.*
>
> *Do you remember that day at the apartment, the day where I ended up pinned under him? I thought he was going to hurt me – or worse. But I kept quiet, I and signed the license at your wedding, thinking that maybe he would change.*
>
> *I'm afraid of what he might do to you.*
>
> *You are someone I admire, who showed me that there was more to life than just existing.*

*This situation has done nothing but agitate me
for the entire time you've been gone, and I won't
do it anymore. I'm washing my hands of you
and your husband. But remember that I love you,
and whatever you do – please, please be careful.*

*Your friend and sister always,
Mattie*

The letter sat on the clipboard overnight, giving her the chance to rescind what she had said. But she didn't, instead walking it down to the mailbox the next morning. She did write a second copy of it at the beginning of a plain, hardcover notebook. At the time she couldn't explain why, but she felt that it was important to keep a record of what she had done.

Helen was lying on her stomach on the living room floor, her son's favorite blanket spread out underneath her as she played with him. It was a small quilt depicting a barnyard, made with painstaking detail by her best friend. Paul was contented to sit underneath a dangling plastic ball that jingled when he managed to hit it. But the room was hot, so she left him momentarily to get up and let in some fresh air.

She gazed out across the grey, faded parking lot as she opened the window, spying the red and white Canada Post truck as it pulled in from the main street. Her days were always busy caring for Paul and passed quickly, but she still waited with baited breath for the mail. Most of the time it was bills, but occasionally she would get a letter from her mother or sister in the States. She kept herself busy until she noticed the truck pulling away, then packed her son onto her hip and carried him downstairs to the mailbox.

Once back upstairs, she shifted her son to her other hip and sorted through the envelopes, tossing them onto the table. There was the power bill and a flyer for the local video store. Her heart leapt when she spied a return address that she had been hoping to see for a long time. Once Paul was back on the floor and occupied, she settled down into a nearby chair to start reading. Tears of anger filled her eyes by the second paragraph. "That bitch…" she muttered to herself. Her volume grew every time she said it. "That fucking bitch."

A few hours later Kevin walked through the door, stopping to look around the living room when he saw the missing frames. "Where'd our wedding pictures go?"

"I put them away," Helen muttered as she shuffled from one side of the room to the other, picking up toys.

He dropped his keys into the dish on top of the stereo stand. "What'd you do that for?"

"I wanted to change some things," she muttered, still not bothering to stop as she cleaned up.

He watched her for a moment, not quite understanding what was eating her. "Well put them back," he told her.

Now she finally stopped, her arms filled with stuffed animals as she stared at him. "Why?"

"Because I like them there." He walked over and gave her a kiss. "They remind me of you." Then he headed into the bathroom to wash his hands.

Helen stared at the spaces where the frames had been and sighed. She had always been sad that they had managed to never take photos of just the two of them that day, but now she cursed it. Mattie was going to haunt her no matter what.

Chapter 24

Mattie's dream of a new day job finally came true, and at the beginning of June she started working as a personal secretary to the manager of a commercial lending firm. The increase in pay made her life a lot easier, not to mention leaving her evenings and weekends free. This in turn facilitated her freedom to start occasionally singing with Zack's band. She didn't feel completely comfortable with their musical style, but the stage experience was invaluable.

As Mattie put her key into the lock of her apartment door, she could hear the telephone ringing inside. With a muttered curse the door finally opened, allowing her to dash to where the phone was hanging. "Hello?"

"Hi."

She recognized Jennifer's voice immediately. "Hey, what's up?" she asked, wandering into the kitchen to unload her grocery bags.

On the other end of the line, Jennifer was dying to tell her best friend her news. "What are you doing right now?"

Mattie opened the cupboard door and put the box of lasagna noodles she had just bought up on the top shelf. "I just got home. Why?"

"My parents are taking Les and I out to celebrate," Jennifer explained, "and I want you to come with us."

As soon as she heard it Mattie knew that it was something big. When Jennifer wanted to celebrate, it was more than likely over a life changing experience. She put a can of soup on the second shelf and questioned, "What's the occasion?"

The grin that had been on Jennifer's face since she opened her mail that afternoon grew just a little bit wider. "I got accepted to Dalhousie."

Even though Mattie had known it was going to be something significant, for some reason she just hadn't anticipated this. The can of corn in her hand hit the counter with a bang. "You're kidding."

"No, I'm not." She let out a hearty laugh. "We're going to be at the Sweet Shop in half an hour. Meet us there?"

"Sure," Mattie replied slowly. "I'll see you there." She took a few steps around the corner to hang the phone back up, then went back into the kitchen. Her mind started to process the news as she continued to put things away. Mattie had been very happy and excited when Jennifer finally applied, even though the applicant herself felt that the chances of actually being accepted to the school were slim. Both Jennifer and Les, as well as all their friends and family, were planning on them moving south so she could attend the University of Calgary.

The last of the groceries were stored, the thin plastic bags in their holder underneath the sink. She felt an immense amount of pride in her friend's accomplishment, but it was obvious that the decision of their moving hadn't been made yet. Mattie already knew what her advice would be.

As she went to the door to put her shoes back on, she caught a glimpse of herself in the hallway mirror. The roundness of her face disgusted her now, a constant reminder that she was now thirty pounds heavier than she had been when she and Graham lived together. Between the strands of hair that formed her bangs she could see the shadows that outlined her blemished forehead, and she cursed again. Lately, it didn't seem to matter what she did – where her body was concerned, she was not getting anywhere. She let out a heavy sigh, thinking to herself for the hundredth time that everyone seemed to be moving forward, while she continued to slide back.

The door slammed shut, leaving Mark standing alone in the corridor.

She had actually thrown him out.

When Sasha started chemotherapy, she stated in no uncertain terms that she didn't want him involved. She would arrange her own transportation for her treatments, but he was not wanted. Her pride didn't want him to see the pain being inflicted on her, especially after he admitted his feelings of guilt for finding the lump. That pride hit a vicious, sarcastic note when she informed him that she didn't want to make him feel any worse than he already did, which was right before she threw him out of the room.

And so he stood there – alone – wondering why he had decided to come here. It felt necessary, but not out of desperation or a need to support her. It was expected – of him and by him – by everyone that knew them. Over the past few weeks, he had started to wonder just exactly how he loved her.

They were well past the lust stage of their relationship, settling into comfortable companionship after she moved in with him. *Comfortable companionship...* As soon as the words appeared in his mind, Mark had his answer. He liked to think that if she had been well, he would have seriously considered leaving her to start all over again.

But she wasn't well. She was fighting breast cancer. And as long as she was contending with that, he would not add to her growing list of problems. Mark heaved a sigh, casting one last glance at the closed door before trudging down to the parkade.

Chapter 25

Dear El,

Do you remember the night I told you all I wanted in life was pure, animal sex? Well it finally happened. And with Zack, just like you predicted. We've been spending a lot of time together lately, and we discussed it over pizza last night. He knows that there's nothing between Graham and I – he even understands the situation because of women friends that he has.

There's absolutely no romantic entanglement – we've just added a physical aspect to our friendship. It's great. I don't have to worry about treading on feelings – or getting mine tread on.

And it doesn't hurt that he's really good in bed either.

Graham pulled up in front of the main door to Mattie's building and put his car into park. Since the lock on the building's main entrance was still broken, he had considered surprising her by coming right to her door and escorting her downstairs. But he could see her exiting the elevator as he arrived, and smiled unconsciously. She was dressed in a black, low cut shirt and jeans, with a long blue trench coat over all. The sides of her long, dark hair were pulled into a simple clip at the back of her head, and she wore a pair of glasses that he had never seen before.

She climbed into the car and immediately gave him a kiss. "Hi there."

"Hi." While she settled in and pulled on her seatbelt, he started to move out of the parking lot and back into traffic. "So what do you feel like doing tonight?"

Mattie thought about his question, and then came up with, "You feel like mall ratting?"

After some consideration he agreed. "That sounds like a good idea."

They headed off toward West Edmonton Mall, which would still be open for the movie theaters, restaurants and clubs that it contained. As they walked through, they noticed a small group of people clustered around the windows of one of the restaurants, where a celebrity actor's band was playing. They watched for a few minutes before moving on and covering the rest of the mall which they had visited many times before.

When they decided to leave, they were stopped as they passed through the loop of the roller coaster by a security guard. He was going to prevent them from using that particular exit because it was nearly ten o'clock and they were in the process of locking up. She piped up and complained because their car was parked immediately outside the door and that it was only ten to ten. The guard took pity on them and let them out, right into a driving burst of rain. Mattie let out a barrage of curses and complaints as they made a run for it.

Once they were in the car Graham started to laugh. He had just invested in his first set of contact lenses a few months before, and didn't miss any of the headaches that went with glasses. She busied herself with cleaning hers while he pulled out of the mall's massive parking lot. "So now what do you want to do?" he asked her.

Her response was, "Pool?"

A few games sounded like a great idea. But in the next few blocks that he drove, Graham decided that it wasn't something he wasn't interested in after all. "I don't really want to," he told her.

"Well I gave you my idea," she told him, slipping out of her shoes and bracing her feet up on the dash. "You think of something."

He thought for a moment, slowly rounding the next curb and pulling out into the main flow of traffic. "We could go find a park and have sex," he suggested.

"In the rain?" she added with a laugh. He fixed her with a quick glance, and she laughed again at how much emphasis he was putting on something that was never going to happen. "Alright – in the rain." Mattie settled back a little further in the passenger seat. "You know," she said in her usual, easy manner, "this casual sex thing is great," referring to her arrangement with Zack.

"Absolutely," he agreed. "There's nothing wrong with saying you're not the one for me, but you'll do for the moment."

They drove straight east until they reached the first turn that would take them down into the river valley. Mattie knew exactly where they were going. It was a place they had been to before, on at least half a dozen occasions while just cruising around the city. It was a picnic park alongside the river, which came complete with a hiding place underneath the bridge that supported Groat Road. The pouring rain outside made things even darker, and as they pulled into the farthest corner of the park there was no mistaking the glow of another set of headlights.

"Well so much for that," she commented as they drove a slow circle around the other car.

"Looks like someone else has the same idea," he mumbled.

"So what do we do now?"

He smiled as inspiration hit him. "I know just the place."

Mattie was forced back into her seat as he stomped on the gas to tear back out onto the freeway. She watched the city pass by in silence, the kind of quiet that sometimes took overtook them when together in the car. This time they headed off in the direction of her apartment building, but turned off at the last minute into a park that she had never known existed. The car slowed to a crawl; their shelter was underneath the road they had just turned off of. On one side was the support for the bridge, on the other was a sloped bank down to a small creek.

She watched Graham turn the key back in the ignition, and a sudden panic set into her. They had made jokes about getting into this situation for so many years now, but the only thing that ever happened was that her imagination would be set into overdrive. Now he released the clasp of his seatbelt, pushed his seat back, and turned expectantly toward her. The silence was still there, but the atmosphere was aroused. He leaned toward her, and her automatic response was to meet him halfway. His kiss was gentle, careful as he tested exactly how far things were going to go. He found her cold, distant and definitely surprised. But he continued to persuade her, melting her resolve each time he brought her lips to his.

When he pulled away, he left Mattie gasping for breath and at a loss for words. She remembered how long it had been since he'd kissed her with that kind of passion, and she had to remind herself that they were both drunk at that time. But they were here now, sober and awake, secluded in their own little place in the middle of the city. Without another thought she kissed him again, reaching down between them to release her own seatbelt.

He felt the buckle being reeled back off her shoulder and took the cue to pull her close to him. One hand wrapped around her back, while the other held her jaw as he coaxed her mouth open a little further. Her sigh was muffled by him, and she remarked silently to herself how careful he was being now. She then felt his fingers trail up between her shoulders and through her hair, where they managed to open the plain brown clip that held it.

They contacted once or twice before parting again, each pressing their forehead against the other's in order not to break their connection. His fingertips pushed into the hair over her ear, pulling out to the side as he ran through the length of her dark locks. His other hand grasped hers when he found it resting on the console between them, and his eyes never left hers. The hand that had just been playing with her hair came back to caress her cheek, and he softly told her, "You have such beautiful skin."

For a moment she thought about what she could say to that, finding the timing of his compliment rather ironic. After a few moments she burst into a small fit of giggles. "Thank you," she managed to tell him, pulling back a little. She was going to tell him about her musings on this subject, then reconsidered the importance of her complexion at the moment.

"You can probably take your coat off," he suggested.

"Oh yeah." Mattie turned around and fumbled for the latch on her seat, throwing it back to nearly horizontal when she found it. Her long coat made the process of removing it clumsy and a little embarrassing, but she did manage to finally get it off and laid down on her side in order to deposit it into the back seat.

Graham moved in on her before she knew what happened, kissing her as he rolled onto his back and pulled her on top of him. She was starting to let herself go a bit, yet kept a firm awareness of every minute detail of what was happening. The awkward position he had put her into started to put a strain on her back, so she pulled away in order to get into a more comfortable position. She knelt on the seat and then hovered above him, her fingers exploring his face. They stopped when he emitted a small, peculiar growl. She looked at him a second before she remarked, "You're purring."

He did it again as he ran his hands through her hair. "You like?"

"I don't know," she shrugged. "I've never heard anyone do that before."

"Don't you do it?"

"No."

"I see." He pulled her lips down to his by wrapping his hand around the back of her head. It was the longest stretch yet and again discomfort caused her to break it off. But for a moment, she lingered to look into his eyes again. He told her, "If we keep going like this, I may not be able to stop."

Scared, Mattie suddenly found her back pressed against the cold glass of the passenger window. Graham sat up, reaching out toward her to let her know that what she'd heard was not what he had meant. She joined him again, this time laying back on her own leather seat. He followed her down, but Mattie's eyes flew open when she felt his hand lightly travel down the front of her shirt. He sensed the shift in her mood as his hand continued to move. She was stretched out along the seat, her right foot braced up against the dashboard. His hand rested on her thigh, and he looked her straight in the eye. "Can I ask you something? And I want you to give me an honest answer."

"Okay?"

"How far do you want to go with this?"

She was suddenly once again aware of the tightness that had filled her stomach when they first parked. When he made the comment about not being able to stop it had set her on edge, but now for some reason, she didn't want to disappoint him. Her answer was simply, "I don't know."

Her nervousness was obvious. So he gently offered, "Just some horsing around?"

The suggestion put her at ease again, and a smile spread across her lips. "Teenager kind of stuff?"

"Yeah."

She reached up and put her arms around him when he leaned down to kiss her, softly at first. A fit of enthusiasm grabbed him, and he pushed his arms under her back and pulled her tight up against his chest. He pressed down hard against her, enough to pinch her bottom lip between their teeth. She thought about saying something, then shook it off and let herself get swept up in the moment.

Graham set her back down again, continuing to kiss her as his hands came around to caress her cheek. She was very aware of that hand as it slowly slid down her chest again. He pulled away, and as he looked into her eyes he grinned. "It's been a long time since my hand was here."

She laughed, reaching up for him again as she agreed, "A long time."

His fingers continued to explore the front of her shirt, then backed up and repeated the motion over the area just below the neckline. "You've got something on your shirt," he commented.

A momentary fit of dread gripped her, as it always did when she managed to miss her mouth at dinner. "What?" she questioned, her eyes scouring what she could see of the black material.

"Embroidery stuff," he said as he continued to brush his hand over the threaded design.

"Oh yeah," she laughed, and reminded him, "That's always been there."

Graham smiled, lifting her chin to look into her eyes. "Come here."

There was only one small kiss before he pulled back. "What?" she questioned.

"These." He carefully pulled the glasses from her face, folded the arms down and set them on the dashboard. "Now I know what I've been doing to all the women I've dated."

They settled into a strong and zealous rhythm for the next while, each delighting in finally being held in the arms of the other. Mattie couldn't help but lose herself to him now, and in the flicker of thought that she gave to the circumstances, she didn't care. For once they were alone, devoid of any distraction aside from each other. As she kissed him, she felt her hope renewing.

As he felt her lips against his and her skin underneath his hands, Graham felt his years lightening and falling away. This was the perfect solution for the itch of mid-life crisis that he had been feeling lately – a younger woman who brought fresh eagerness into his life. Her hair wrapped easily around his fingers, and as he stroked the strands his mental image of her was beginning to change. He started to see women from his past, the image that remained the longest being Kim. It still hurt. Though his eyes were already closed, his vision darkened even further as he started to imagine that she was there with him now, not years before when those sensations had been real.

In the short break between soft, easy songs on the radio, a station identification announcement came on that remarked, *"Songs playing in the front seat while you were playing in the back seat"*.

Mattie lost it and burst out laughing. He grinned at her and remarked, "We were doing so well, too." Their foreheads rested against each other, one's eyes never wavering from the other's. Graham reached up to run his fingers through the hair over her ear, and as soon as he touched her she nuzzled her cheek into his palm. "For someone who doesn't purr," he said softly, "you seem to be doing pretty well."

They reached a mutual and wordless agreement to slow down for a while, so she laid back down against his chest while he sat up in the driver's seat. Her eyes closed, and she now realized that she had found the place that all her married friends had told her about – the place in the world where she felt safe. Behind her, he pulled her tight and listened attentively as she hummed along with the radio. Until she abruptly stopped. He asked, "Whatcha thinking?"

"About everybody leaving," she said with a sigh.

"What do you mean?"

She absently stroked the arm that held her in place as she started to think out loud. "Well, Adam has already gone to Toronto, and Jennifer is moving to Halifax at the end of the month. And Helen..." The words caught in her throat, a rush of emotion threatening to overwhelm her.

Graham looked down at her, suddenly uncomfortable. It occasionally tugged at his heart when he saw her cry, but he was never sure of what he should be doing. "You miss her, don't you?"

"It's so frustrating, you know," she continued, not hearing what he had said. "It just seems like I'm not going anywhere. I don't know what I'm going to do with my life."

A rare moment of compassion finally struck her best friend and he whispered, "You're going to be just fine."

Tears welled up in her eyes, and she inadvertently let out a sniffle as she tried to get her emotions under control. But for as high as they were running now, it was impossible. He comforted her by hugging her even more tightly, leaning down to kiss the top of her head. *If you only knew how long I've been waiting for you to say that,* she thought to herself.

It was then that fate decided to intervene. Well, actually it was the cops, who kicked us out of the park because it was closed. And just when things were getting interesting.

We drove around for a little while longer, but it was pretty obvious that the moment was gone. So Graham drove me home.

They parked outside her front door, but neither was ready to say goodnight quite yet. "You're coming to Les and Jennifer's going away party, aren't you?" she asked.

He nodded, "Absolutely."

"Great." She hit him with a deeply passionate kiss, picking up from where they had left off underneath the bridge.

Graham pulled away somewhat abruptly and warned, "You know, we're out in the open now."

"Yeah, I know." She kissed him again, the past few hours fuelling her bravado. And when she was done, she quietly informed him, "I love you, you know."

Her admission visibly shook him, and it suddenly occurred to him that they may have embarked on something more than just releasing the sexual tension that had filled their relationship since the start. After what they had been up to for the past couple of hours, he really wasn't sure what to say next. He opted to whisper back a tentative, "I love you."

Her expression remained unchanged. She knew it was coming, and she knew exactly how much truth there was behind it right now. "Goodnight," was all she said before getting out and closing the passenger door behind her. Graham watched her through the lobby windows until she stepped inside the elevator, and then headed for home with his mind in a whirl.

Chapter 26

Despite an aggressive regimen and the care of one of the best oncologists in the country, Sasha was losing her battle. The cancer spread into her lymph nodes within a matter of weeks. And as soon as she received that news, Sasha's survival instinct started to die too. No amount of encouragement, from her parents or from Mark, was able to penetrate the self-pity that was consuming her. She finally allowed her boyfriend to help her from day to day, but she still refused to let him in.

He wanted to bring her home, to comfort her for however many days she had left. But she was resistant – their condo really had never truly felt like home for her. Her mother's boss owned a summer house on the coast which he graciously offered to the couple for as long as they needed it. Mark was surprised when Sasha agreed, but took it with a grain of salt. It seemed that every step forward with her would mean that the inevitable three steps back were sure to follow. She still would not see anyone, not even her family, and would keep all the drapes drawn to keep out the light.

Mark came back to the house during the middle of the day, drawing a deep breath before abandoning the sunshine to go inside. It was quiet, the air fresh from the sea as it blew past the unusually opened curtains, and for the first time he noticed the bright and airy design of the house. But something didn't feel right, and his throat constricted as he started to creep through the rest of the house. He carefully stepped into the bedroom, stopping for a moment to let his eyes adjust. This room was still dark, the sun muted by the thick curtains that ran across the window. The radio on the dresser was softly tuned to a country station, and Sasha was motionless in bed.

He sat down on the edge of the mattress, far enough away so as not to disturb her. Her body was in a prone position, her pale cheek resting on top of her right hand. There was no problem hearing her breathe, but each time she exhaled, he was terrified that it would be the last. After ten minutes of watching, he smiled sheepishly to himself and decided that there was still a little time left. His stomach emitted a loud, urgent growl, reminding him that he hadn't eaten since the night before. He carefully got up, only taking a couple of steps toward the door when he heard her say, "Don't go."

He stopped short, slowly turning around and seeing that she was gazing at him with tired eyes. Mark pasted what he thought was an encouraging smile on his face. "How long have you been awake?" he asked as he sat back down beside her.

"Since before you got here," she replied, allowing her eyes to slowly close again.

"Why didn't you say anything?"

"I just wanted to be with you for a while." Sasha lifted her head as she reached out for him, and once his hands held hers, she fell back against the pillow. "No words, no crying. Just you."

He frowned. "Have you been crying?"

"I was," she said with a weak nod. "But I can't anymore."

To himself, Mark remarked about how right she was. To her he questioned, "What were you crying about?"

"You."

"Me?"

Sasha nodded again. "I was imagining what your life will be like without me in it."

He drew an uncomfortable breath, not really sure if he wanted to know what she had been thinking. It was hard enough thinking of it himself. "What did you see?" he finally asked.

Her eyes closed a little tighter as she remembered. "You were sitting at my funeral," she started, "with Duffy and Tamora. You didn't show any emotion at all, never let yourself grieve for me. And then you were all alone, with only Jack to keep you company." Sasha suddenly drew in a sharp breath, enough to shift her position on the mattress.

"Sasha?" He moved up beside her, sudden alarm filling his voice. "Sasha?"

She waved him off, then laid a hand on his knee when the difficulty passed. "I'm okay," she assured him, her voice a little hoarse. "I'm not leaving yet."

"Sorry." Eventually Mark laid down and pulled her into his arms, absently wondering how many more times he'd be able to do it.

They lapsed into a long stretch of silence, each just listening to the other breathe. Eventually Sasha whispered a confession. "I know that you're not in love with me anymore, Mark. But I know that you do still love me. You can't know just how grateful I am for that." She shuddered in his arms. "I'm so sorry I pushed you away."

He just stroked her downy hair for a while, but eventually murmured, "So am I."

Graham wandered around the crowded bazaar that surrounded the city's summer theater festival. Most of the stalls sold more or less the same stock of trinkets and clothing; this year, the hot purchase was tie-dyed cotton shirts. The knapsack that he had been carrying all day on his back was growing unbearably heavy, compounding the discomfort inside his beat-up sneakers. He decided that he needed to take a load off, so he veered off from the main crowd into one of the beer tents.

The drinking area was just as packed as the rest of the bazaar, loud and rowdy under the patio lights that lit the inside of the tent. He looked around for someone that he knew, but found no one either inside or on the fenced-in patio. There was, however, someone behind the makeshift bar that he hadn't seen since the festival the year before.

There were three people there, one selling drink tickets while the other two filled orders. The plain woman selling tickets was the one that he remembered. Graham swaggered up to the right side of the table, nonchalantly rested his arm up on the small podium that formed the kiosk and said, "Hello Beautiful."

Rhonda Harper was not the least bit impressed with his sudden appearance, but it didn't bother her either. They had met the summer before in the same beer tent, under the exact same circumstances. But that night, she had found out that her best friend had stolen the man that she was interested in dating; by the time that she was supposed to meet Graham for a drink after her shift, she had decided to vent her frustrations by going three rounds with a cinder block wall. They had kept in loose contact for a couple of months afterwards, then eventually nothing. "How ya doin' Graham?" she greeted as she continued to hand out tickets.

"I'm good."

For a reason she couldn't explain, Rhonda felt the need to be polite, so she carried the conversation on. "So what brings you down here?"

"Just wasting time." He nodded to a casual acquaintance that passed by. "I'm meeting somebody in a little while."

"And who's that?"

"Oh, nobody special." He checked his watch at the mention of meeting Mattie. "Listen, you wanna get a drink after your shift?"

There was a short pause as she served another customer. "Well some friends and I are getting together once I'm done. You're welcome to join us."

Graham's face lit up with the possibility of seeing her again that night. "Sure. What time?"

"'Bout half an hour."

He grinned at her. "That sounds great. I'll see you then." He turned around and wandered back out into the fray.

"Who was that?" the woman serving drinks asked Rhonda.

"Just someone I met last year," she confirmed. "He's no big deal."

In the small park that sat in the middle of the festival site, a large crowd had gathered to watch a rambunctious juggling comedy troupe that had taken over the gazebo. It was early enough in the evening that there were a great number of children in the audience, yet late enough that the outdoor venue had to be lit from large towering scaffolds. Mattie lingered at the southwestern edge of the crowd, her attention flitting between the jugglers and the crowd that passed by on the other side. She checked her watch again – it was nearly ten. Her shoulders heaved with an impatient huff of air as she surveyed the area again. He was definitely late. Impatience finally got the better of her, forcing her to turn around to watch the show.

Graham wound his way through an oncoming crowd, its density twice as thick as it had been when he went into the beer tent. A large cheer went up from the gazebo, which started him on trying to look for Mattie as he approached their prearranged meeting spot. He was nearly to the end of the small alley that formed the bazaar when he saw what he thought looked like the back of her. Never one to pass up an opportunity, he sneaked up behind her and clamped a hand down on her shoulder.

"Jesus Christ!" she half-shrieked, jumping out from under his fingers. She spun around, fire flickering through her eyes when she confronted him. "What the hell is wrong with you?"

He couldn't help but grin. "Did I scare you?"

"D'ya think? Jerk." She shook her head and readjusted her bag. "Where have you been?"

"Sorry. I got caught up at the beer tent." He leaned down to give her a quick greeting kiss.

"Come on. We're gonna be late for the show." She started to leave, but he caught her by the arm to keep her from going. Her brow furrowed as she tried to figure out what he was up to. "What?"

"I just came to tell you that I can't make it." Mattie folded her arms over her chest and hit him with her unflinching stare. "Something's come up," he said, trying to remain both nonchalant and non-specific. "Change in plans."

His friend continued to glare at him for a while before she flatly asked, "Who is she, Graham?"

Caught, he gave her a sheepish grin. "Somebody I met here last year. We're going for a beer after her shift is finished."

"Thanks a lot."

"For what?"

The magnitude of his ignorance astounded her most days, but even she couldn't believe how it stepped up every once in a while. "It didn't dawn on you that you had already made plans with me?" she reminded him.

In an attempt to gain a little sympathy, he played up the guilt factor and started to dig his toe into the soft ground. The first and most convenient excuse he could come up with was, "I guess I just forgot."

"Like I said, thanks a lot." The sarcasm was thick between them, her clear indicator that he wasn't out of the doghouse. Not by a long shot.

Graham considered his options. "I can break it if you want..."

"Go," she sighed in resignation. "One of us should have a date this year. It may as well be you."

He grinned with delight. "Thanks." After another quick kiss, he vanished back into the throng.

Mattie watched him as he disappeared, and resisted the temptation to fling an offensive gesture in his direction. Now she was stuck with his ticket to the show that she really didn't even want to see – he had convinced her to go with him. *Why do I let him get away with this shit?* she asked herself as she turned back to the show. But by this time the performance was over, the jugglers holding out their hats and thanking people as they dropped coins into them. "Oh for Christ's sake," she muttered under her breath. She dumped the pair of tickets into the first hat that passed by, and then joined the wave of people that was headed in her direction. He would pay for the tickets later.

Chapter 27

In passing conversation, Mattie had mentioned rudimentary plans for the going away party to another couple she knew, Rob and Joanne Thompson. Being generous people, they felt free to offer their hosting services for a couple that they had only met a handful of times. Mattie was thankful beyond belief, and once a good location was established and all the guests knew where the party was, Mattie threw herself into the preparations.

The day finally arrived three weeks later, and Mattie went to their house late in the afternoon to help set up. She picked up the mix and decorations on the way, and when she stepped through the back gate she found Rob racing in one direction or another, from the yard to the house and back again. It was enough to make Mattie dizzy. "What can I do?" she asked as she followed him into the house.

Unbelievably, he stopped for a moment to think – but he was moving again before he even started talking. "Can you get all the burger stuff ready for me?" He retrieved industrial size jars of relish, peppers and pickles from the fridge, along with a pair of large white onions and carried them over to the counter on the other side of the room. "Just slice up the pickles and onions…" He grabbed four wooden dishes from the cupboard, "and put everything into bowls."

"Sure." He immediately left her alone to tend to other matters, and as she started her work, she began to hum. The blues album that she had been listening to for the last week was foremost in her mind, so as she tied her hair back she started to sing to herself. The back door was slamming shut almost continuously as Rob continued to run around, either getting something for the barbecue or for his young son. As she was dicing onions she heard the door open again, but not the hurried footsteps that usually went with it. "These are just about ready for you to take outside," she called without turning away from the cutting board. Her senses picked up a little when no answer came, and she purposely went back to singing the last song that she had been listening to in the car.

The melody cut off abruptly when Graham's arms slid around her waist and a soft kiss touched the back of her neck, just where it met her shoulder. He lingered there for a moment or two before leaning around her, where she had turned to kiss him in greeting. Glancing at what she was doing, he asked her, "Why aren't you crying?"

Mattie frowned. "What?"

He smiled, glancing down at the onions. "Everybody cries when they chop onions. How do you do that?"

"I breathe through my mouth." She turned back to her work, scooping up small bits of onion with her hand and the knife and pouring them into one of the bowls. "Did you bring the ice?" she asked.

"It's already in the tub in the garage," he reported.

"Good. I want everything to be perfect tonight."

He took her by the shoulders, turning her toward him so he could kiss her again before quietly assuring her, "It will be."

Hours later, Mattie sat on the back step of Rob and Joanne's house, just watching everyone around her. Jennifer and Les were busy chatting with their friends, the center of attention. Tears started to fill Mattie's eyes, but she blinked them away before they could fall. She had promised herself she wouldn't cry, so her goodbye speech to her friends had been short and sweet to avoid any kind of emotional outburst. For now she was just content to fade into the background and let the couple enjoy their evening. There would be plenty of time to feel lonely later.

Joanne stopped at the bottom of the steps, carrying a tray full of leftover paper plates and plastic forks. "Can you give me a hand?"

"Yeah sure." Mattie scrambled to her feet to open the door, then followed Joanne up into the kitchen.

"You've been awfully quiet tonight," Joanne pointed out as she watched Mattie take items from her overloaded arms and set them down on the counter.

"Yeah," Mattie said with a nod. "Keeps me from bawling."

"I can understand that." Joanne started putting the loose forks and knives back into the plastic bags that they had been bought in. Then she asked, "So what's with you and Graham?"

Mattie gave a half-smile, glad to finally have someone she could confide in. When she had tried to tell Jennifer about what had happened under the bridge, her friend had reacted with revulsion. She told Mattie that she couldn't understand why she would do something like that with somebody who was so obviously beneath her. Zack had taken it upon himself to remind her of all the cold, heartless things that Graham had ever done to her. Mattie had listened to them, but their words only deepened the guilt that she felt over the fact that she still was attracted to him after all of his flaws were pointed out. "I don't know," she mused. "The past couple months he's stopped acting like a friend and started acting like....well, like a lover."

Joanne looked at her, her eyebrows raised in interest. "A lover?"

"Uh huh," the other nodded. "It's weird."

"Do you think it's going to go anywhere?"

Out of all the thought that Mattie had put into what had been happening with Graham, neither she nor anyone else had posed that question. After some thought she said, "I don't know. He acts like he's in love with me, but he keeps talking about this girl he met back at Fringe. Rhonda – I think…It's getting really annoying."

Joanne twisted the top of the bag shut and secured it with a green tie. "Have you said anything to him about it?" she asked.

"Not yet. We haven't really had a chance to talk all week."

Rob came back inside, leaning up the stairs to stick his head into the kitchen. "Les and Jennifer are leaving," he told them. "You gonna come say goodbye?" The two women followed him back outside, where the guests of honor were collecting hugs and well wishes from all of their friends. Mattie still remained back from the crowd, not wishing to get involved now. She would have her own opportunity to say goodbye the day they actually left.

It didn't take long for the party to break up and despite Mattie's offers, Rob and Joanne said they would clean up and let her off for the night. Graham offered to walk her home – and though it was a long stretch, she accepted, especially since she had had a few drinks that night. For a while they walked, trading pleasantries but not really hitting any specific topic. On the last block before her building, one of the street lamps had burned out. Graham suddenly interrupted her in mid-sentence by announcing, "Dark spot!" and in one fluid motion he grabbed her hand, whirled her around to pull her up against him and kissed her hard.

Momentarily stunned, she gasped, "What was that for?"

He shrugged. "Just a thought." She fixed him with a funny look, so he moved in for another kiss. But she ducked him and continued back down their original path. He stopped to light a cigarette, then trotted to catch up.

They made it about halfway down the block and turned at the entrance to the building complex. She swallowed hard, then ventured, "So what's the deal with you and Rhonda?"

There was a marked silence between them. "I don't know," he told her. "I haven't seen her since Fringe, so there is no deal as yet." Graham frowned as something occurred to him. "Why? You jealous?"

Mattie wasn't sure of the best way to respond to his challenge. Finally she opted for, "What would you say if I said yes?"

"I thought so."

She reached for the door handle, but was stopped when he rested his hand on top of hers. Her eyes demanded an explanation, and Graham blew the smoke out of his lungs before asking her, "Can I walk you to your door?"

Mattie did a double take, not quite sure that she had heard what she thought he said. There was a little bit of nervousness in her response, prompted by curiosity at his request. "Sure."

As they stepped into the elevator his tension eased, and as she watched the floors pass he stole a look at her. She was purposely keeping her distance from him, trying to gain the upper hand. The look became a stare, limited only by the length of time needed to reach to the fifth floor. Without really noticing it himself, he was starting to see attractions in her which until then had eluded him.

Mattie was the first to step out into the hallway, keys jingling in her hand as she walked. For a half second she thought about stopping at the door for the classic movie goodnight kiss. But being so familiar with each other, they wordlessly made it inside. She dropped her purse on the floor in its usual place just as Max appeared at the corner of the hallway. "Hey you," she cooed, kneeling down to scratch him behind the ears. "How's my boy?"

The cat mewed his response, continuing to talk to her as he arched his back to rub against her knee. "What a suck," Graham observed from behind her.

"Of course he is," she reminded him. "There's somebody here." She could sense her friend's mood behind her and was keenly aware that they were still in the dark. Wanting to keep the game in her favor, Max received more attention than he usually did when his human got home. But her knees finally began to shake under her weight and she was forced to straighten up. "I still say I want to be a housecat in my next life," she said as she started to turn around.

Unable to contain his want any longer, Graham locked her into a strong embrace before she could say anything else. Her apprehension at being suddenly grabbed melted away with a second or two of his convincing, giving way to an aggressive sort of behavior that neither of them ever would have expected from her. His kisses broke away from her mouth and worked their way back to her ear, which prompted a low growl from the back of her throat. He pulled away. "What was that?"

She gazed at him in the limited light and smiled. "Purring." Her hand reached up and started to stroke the stubble that covered his jaw and neck, making him arc his back against the door. His head fell back against the door, his eyes sliding shut at the touch of her fingertips on his neck. Again and again she brushed over his skin, combing through his moustache on several occasions. Graham reveled in her attention until he couldn't tolerate any more of her teasing. He caught her fingers in a strong but gentle grip, folded them over the top of his hand and started to kiss them.

She watched him with fascination, never having experienced affection quite like this. Her fingers straightened at his silent request, and once again he brought them to his mouth. When he was sufficiently distracted she stood on her toes to start kissing his neck, though her lack of height forced her to pull him forward so she could reach him. Eventually she ended up bent half over backwards, taking him with her all the way.

Twenty minutes passed before he reluctantly broke their connection. "I should get going," he whispered, not really fighting her when she continued to kiss him.

"No you don't," she murmured, pressing her forehead to his. "Stay."

It worked for a little while, but eventually he firmed his position. "I really do have to go," he told her. "Sleep well." They kissed once more, then she helped him unlock the door so that he could go out into the hallway. Before starting for the elevator, he turned back and told her, "I love you."

"I love you too." She watched him walk away and out of her sight before closing the door. The last time he had used that particular phrase, it had been only in response to her saying it first – the result of pure shock. But now it sounded sincere and honest. Once again, just when she thought she had figured things out, everything was tossed to hell, and their brief discussion of Rhonda was long forgotten.

"You did what?"

Mattie's eyes slid shut, her lover's disgust resonating in her ears as she again repeated what she had said. Zack rolled over to face her, frowning at her indiscretion. "I thought you said that you were over that."

"I thought I was," she admitted, feeling a sudden need to cover up and pulling the quilt up under her chin. "But Graham's been acting really different lately."

Her neighbor pushed his disapproval aside as he propped himself up on an elbow. "How so?"

In her mind Mattie considered the whole situation, particularly the times that she and Graham had been quite intimate. Originally she had opted not to tell Zack, but he had noticed that something was weighing on her mind and wouldn't leave her alone until she talked it out with him. So she sketched out the details for him, ending the tale with, "I mean, come on. How many friends ask if they can walk you to your door?"

After a while Zack questioned, "Do you think it would work?"

"No." She heaved a sigh of frustration and became lost in thought, but Zack shifting his weight on the mattress brought her back into the moment. She could see the look that he was giving her, so she added, "But I have to know."

Zack frowned and shook his head. "Whatever you think is best." Then he climbed up and suspended himself on his arms over top of her. "Can I 'walk you to your door'?" he asked, a wicked smile on his lips as he slowly removed the blanket that covered her.

"That's not funny," she scolded through her laughter. Giggles turned into satisfied moans as he started to work at her neck and down the front of her body. But despite his attentions, her thoughts really didn't leave the subject of their discussion.

Chapter 28

I am an idiot, El.

What could have ever possibly convinced me that Graham actually loved me? Or at least loved me in the way I wanted him to?

I saw him with Rhonda today at the mall. He doesn't know I saw him – I just happened to be there to pick up the pictures I took at Les and Jennifer's party.

I followed him.

It was so obvious that he's in love with her, plain enough even for me to see. And seeing him kiss her was enough to confirm it. I couldn't watch anymore. I started crying as soon as I got into my car and didn't stop for hours. Poor Zack ran into me in the hallway - his shirt will never be the same.

This is the end. But the worst part, more than losing him, is that I'm terrified. I've thought about this off and on for more than a year now, and I'm so scared that I'm being stupid. I don't want to lose another best friend.

Despite her best efforts to avoid him, Mattie realized that Graham was inextricably linked to almost every facet of her life. A few weeks later, he turned up at a bar where she had volunteered to sing for a charity fundraiser, and when she spied him from the stage her heart nearly stopped. It took everything she had to continue her performance of a difficult Janis Joplin number. She would have liked nothing better than to walk off stage there and then, or to at least dive in behind the drum kit and hide.

She made sure she was surrounded by people at each break so that he would have no access to her. But he unwaveringly sidestepped the exiting crowd to approach her after her last set was complete, his usual grin in full force. "You sound good," he told her, kissing her in greeting. "But I don't know if you should be doing Joplin."

Mattie exchanged an exasperated glance with Zack, who was discretely listening from his place behind Graham while he packed up equipment. "Always a critic," she muttered, daggers in her eyes. "If you want to heckle, go to the Laugh Pit."

The comment in itself was not unusual for her, but for once Graham actually realized that there was meaning behind it. He did a brief double take, but pushed it aside and offered, "Can I drive you home?"

Mattie shook her head. "We're going to go out for breakfast," she told him, indicating the rest of the band behind her.

Zack stood up as soon as he heard her say it. "Actually, I promised that I would stop by my friend's birthday party," he told them.

The rest of the band also offered their excuses of wives, children or various other commitments. Mattie absently wondered if Zack had blatantly arranged a situation that she wouldn't be able to get out of to make her face Graham and end things once and for all. Left with no alternative and no lie, she felt helpless without Zack's ride home. "Alright," she agreed reluctantly.

He grinned and swept his arm toward the door. "Your chariot awaits."

Mattie shot Zack a dirty look as Graham led her toward the exit. Zack simply shrugged, knowing full well what he had done for her.

The car parked in its customary place in front of her building and was automatically shut off. Graham smiled as he turned to her, running his fingertip along the side of her cheek. "Can I walk you to your door?" he asked.

For a split second Mattie considered his offer, ready to fall back into the same comfortable void that she always found herself in when in his company. But then she remembered what she saw in the mall two days before, and her heart constricted. With a shake of her head she softly told him, "I don't think so."

She had fought to keep her tone even and neutral – it didn't fool him one bit. Her expression was one of stone, and what may have been unreadable to some was telltale to him. "What did I do?"

Her eyes flew from the parking lot in front of the car to the man who sat in the driver's seat. Everything welled up inside her at once – their old fights, her love for him and her frustration at its unrequited quality. She remembered singing at his parents' piano when they first started spending time together, and feeding the pigeons in Trafalgar Square with him four years later. The events of their first major fight came back and brought all their anger with them, magnified by the intensity of her remorse in being drawn back to him twice since then. In her mind, Mattie started to list all of the responses to his question that she had thought of over the years – ones that she had never got to use because he had never asked the question. So no one was more surprised than her when all that came out of her mouth was, "Nothing." Their eyes locked for just a moment, and then she curtly ended things with, "Goodnight."

Graham only had the small amount of time it took for her to close the passenger door to make up his mind. Usually the best thing to do when Mattie got like this was to leave her alone and allow things to blow over. She would return to her normal self soon after and this incident likely would never be mentioned again. It was an indescribable force that pulled him out onto the asphalt. She was nearly through the outer door of the building when he called after her, "Wait!"

She ignored him, instead blazing through the lobby and into the conveniently open elevator. Once on her own floor, she slammed the apartment door behind her, pausing for a moment before she hurled her purse against the far wall. She swiped the pack of cigarettes off the coffee table as she stormed by, lighting one as she stepped out onto the balcony. "Jackass," she muttered to herself between puffs.

He came barreling out into her sanctuary almost immediately. "Now just a goddamn minute…"

She whirled around, finding Graham standing in the doorway. "What the…?" Then she cursed inwardly, realizing not only that she hadn't locked the door behind her, but that the landlord still hadn't fixed the lock on the security door downstairs. "Get out of here!"

"No. Not until we settle this."

Mattie turned her back on him. "There's nothing to settle."

He followed her out onto the balcony, anger rising in his voice. "If I did something wrong, I at least have the right to know what it is!"

She took another pull from her cigarette, purposely staring out across the river valley, one arm folded across her torso as she continued to smoke. "What do you care?"

He grabbed her elbow and spun her around. "For Christ's sake, what did I do that was so wrong?"

"It's what you didn't do!" she spat at him, the cigarette tumbling onto the concrete below as she wrenched herself from his grip.

"What the hell does that mean?"

She couldn't believe that he was going to stand there and play stupid. "You didn't even bother to tell me that you're dating Rhonda."

Graham frowned. "I'm not dating her."

Mattie struck out at him, hitting him squarely in the chest with the heels of both hands. "I saw you! I saw you kissing her!"

The force of her blow sent him back a couple of steps. "I kiss lots of women!"

"No you don't – I've never seen you kiss anyone else."

"So I kissed her," he challenged. "So what?"

"You don't love her!" she yelled at him. "You love me!"

"No I don't!"

His outburst shocked her, leaving her speechless for a few moments. Finally, in a much quieter voice that belied her anger she questioned, "You don't?"

The question took Graham completely by surprise – he hadn't realized what he had said. "Don't what?"

Her head cocked as she stared at him in disbelief. "You don't love me?"

"I..." He tried to set his madly spinning mind in order, looking for what would be the right thing to say. The best he could do was to tell her the truth. Finally. At last. "No," he said quietly, with a tiny shake of his head, "I don't."

Stunned again into silence, Mattie could do nothing but gape at him. She turned away, blinking hard to hold back the tears forming in her eyes. It didn't seem possible, but she felt a bigger fool now than she ever had before. Cold wind whipped around her, barely registering as it tossed her hair into her face. One lone tear escaped, running down her cheek and eventually dropping down onto hands that now gripped the balcony railing.

Beside her, Graham wasn't quite sure what to do. He really hadn't thought about his true feelings for his best friend. He had briefly toyed with the idea of asking her out after their experience around the bonfire years before. And though that had never come to pass, he still valued her as his closest companion. He had never considered her to be more than that. But those feelings had resurged after their evening together under the bridge and he had dutifully buried them deep within himself, knowing full well that he had confused his longings for Kim with the convenience of the woman that was in his life now.

His reverie was broken when he heard her whisper, "How could you?" Mattie looked up at him, now showing the tears that she was no longer able to hide. "You held my hand, you kissed me…tried to make love to me…" She looked out across the valley again. "But it didn't mean anything…did it?"

He was realizing now that he hadn't buried his feelings as completely as he had first thought. But ever in denial, Graham cleared his throat before saying, "It didn't."

Mattie hung her head. He had to strain to hear her when she told him, "You can't just love me when it's convenient, Graham." After noticing the way he was looking at her, she added, "You start to let yourself go and live in the moment, but then you catch yourself and push me away."

"I do not," he countered.

"Yes you do." Mattie blew a huff of air out through her teeth. "You start to act like a lover. You're attentive, you're caring, you're even romantic. But then you get scared – and you treat me like shit." His eyes flicked down, an indicator that her words had hit their mark. "I can't do this," she told him. "I can't keep bouncing at the end of this string you're keeping me on."

Fire flashed in his eyes, resentment being the first thing that flew out of his mouth. "I *never* tried to string you along," he stated.

"That's just it!" she countered before he could continue. "You're not trying. You're not even aware that you're doing it!"

Graham's voice grew lower like it always did when he was mad. "I have never, *ever* done anything to deliberately hurt you."

In contrast, Mattie's pitch was starting climb. "Then who did I see strolling around with Rhonda Harper Thursday night?" She could see his guilt deepening. "Deliberate or not, you still did it." Mattie clutched at the buttons of her blouse when she started off on her new tirade. "Graham, I am not going to stand here and wait for you to figure out whether or not you really love me." She took half a step over and sat down on the nearest chair, clutching her jacket tight around her body to ward off the night's chill. After taking a good dozen controlled breaths to steady herself, she asked him, "Do you remember the night that you and I went out for dinner, the first one after we started talking again?"

He nodded, that particular night actually ingrained quite clearly in his memory. In his mind he was running through the disastrous dinner, trying to find the piece that she would focus on. He realized that it wasn't the meal, but the call afterwards that had her attention now. "We were on the phone for hours," he said, hoping that he was on the same wavelength as she was. He took the opportunity to move down and take the chair next to hers.

"I felt like my parents were smothering me," she confirmed, her eyes never leaving him as he sat down. "Do you remember what your advice to me was?"

Graham had to think back, fingers scratching behind his ear as he grasped for the fine details of that conversation. "I said that no matter how much you love someone, you have to cut them loose if they're getting in your way." She looked at him, a lick of her lips replacing the words that she was hesitating to say. His hand dropped back onto his leg with dead weight and he gasped, "I didn't mean me."

Now tears started to flow down Mattie's cheeks again, dripping off her jaw onto her shaking knees. "I have to live my life," she whispered, glancing alternately between his face and the concrete floor below. "There's nothing I would love more than to always have you in it. All you had to do was ask. But I can't go on like this. Maybe if nothing would have happened again after the first time we decided not to...but I want more than that now."

His hand found its way over to rest on her thigh. He was reeling, and though he didn't know exactly what he felt, he was sure that he did not want to let her walk out of his life forever. But he had to tell her, "I can't give you what you want, Mattie."

"I know."

Graham leaned forward and kissed her gently, caressing her cheek in his hand. When they parted he got onto his feet and moved inside, slowly closing the screen behind him. Before he left, he turned around and asked her, "Are you sure?"

Without moving she confirmed, "Yes."

For a moment he considered her answer. "I'm sorry." Soon after, she heard the small click of the door being shut, and she was alone.

As soon as she knew he was gone she really started to cry, uncontrollable jerking sobs that wracked her entire body. Out on the street she saw his black sports car speed away, momentarily breaking her from her anguish. She watched it until it disappeared from sight, and for a long time after, she just looked at the last place she had seen it. Her mind was blank, too tired to replay what had just happened. There would be plenty of time for that later.

The sun was starting to shoot streaks of grey light across the sky when she heard her front door open. She had lost all track of time, and wondered how long she had been sitting there, staring out into the street. Zack appeared in the balcony doorway, checking in both directions to see if she was alone. "I saw your light on." She didn't say anything, her voice choked by the new tears that started rolling down her cheeks. So he knelt down beside her and put his arms around her, just to hold his friend as she cried.

Chapter 29

Mark sat alone on the couch in the corner, desperately wishing everyone would just leave him alone. He had endured just about enough of this outpouring of sympathy. His family, Sasha's family, mutual friends and acquaintances...more people than he could remember seeing in a long time. With a sigh, he vaguely wondered where they all had been when Sasha lay on her deathbed a few days before.

His eyes flicked up to the coffin on the other side of the room. Her mother had insisted on an open casket, and though he couldn't understand why, he had complied with her wishes. The viewing room of the funeral home was packed, but he didn't see any of them. He saw her pale skin, contrasting with closed eyes painted with too much makeup and hair so sparse that it barely covered her head. Many people gasped at the state of her cancer-ravaged body, hardly believing that it was Sasha Waldron.

But Mark knew better. Despite his initial misgivings, he fulfilled his vow to himself and stayed with her, turning out to be the only one strong enough to be by her side at the end. He had clutched her hand, stroking the back of it with his fingers as he softly encouraged her to let go. She was in a coma for nearly three days before she finally succumbed to the disease that had pretty much defeated her from the start. And he was there the entire time. Most people saw it as a sign of unwavering devotion – a select few, including Sasha herself, knew better.

Mattie folded into herself after Graham left, depression swallowing her. She had tried to go back to work that Monday, but found it impossible to concentrate on anything but her misery. After sticking it out for two days, she conceded defeat and called in sick for the rest of the week.

Zack had visited her many times, trying his best to cheer her up. He thought he had helped her turn a corner when he left for his own job on Friday morning; she had promised to at least get dressed and clean up the apartment by the time he came back to check on her again. He blew in through her door around two that afternoon, peering around each corner at the end of the entrance hall to see where she was at. "Matt?" He stopped short when he saw in the same pajamas that he had left her in that morning. "Have you been here all day?"

She looked down at the pile of tissues and dishes that had built up around both her and Max. "No."

He shook his head. "You can't stay in here forever, you know."

"I know," she told him, balling up the tissue that was in her hand and tossing it across the coffee table. "I'll go to work on Monday."

"That's not what I meant." He managed to find a somewhat clear space near her and sat down. "Matt, you have to get out and do something."

"I don't want to."

"Honey, you've gotta shake this thing."

She fixed him with a funny look. "Wanna fuck?"

"Don't be crude."

"Come on," she tried to encourage.

He shook his head. He'd be trying very hard to get her spirits back up, but she seemed to be resisting him at every turn, and it was getting frustrating. "I'm not sleeping with you when you're like this," he told her, their eyes locking in an uncomfortable glare.

The sound of the mail carrier in the hallway was the perfect excuse to break the tension. "Mail!" he cried as he leapt from the couch and headed for the stack of letters that had been pushed through the slot in the door. He sorted through the envelopes as he walked back in, trying to be funny as he recited, "Bills...bills...bills..."

"Oh give me those." She snatched her mail out of his hands, finding herself actually interested in the contents as she flipped through them. One envelope stood out from all the rest, halfway between a standard size window envelope and a manila folder. The neatly printed label jumped out at her, as well as the lack of a return address.

"What's that?" he asked, watching her pull it out to take a look.

"I have no idea." The rest of the mail landed in disarray on the couch and the floor in front of her, the envelope turning over and over in her hands as she searched it for clues as to the sender. Finally curiosity forced her to open it, but her confusion only grew when she pulled out a burned CD with no labeling. She held it up to show Zack and shrugged her confusion.

He took the CD from her and slid it into her stereo to play. The recording sounded homemade as well, with a distinct hum in the background as a piano started to play. Mattie listened intently, eager to know why it had been sent to her. But when Graham's thin voice started to sing the lyrics, it nearly stopped her heart. His first attempt at songwriting had been rough, but it got its point across as the main line of the chorus chanted again and again.

"All you had to do was ask..."

Zack had spent the song staring at the CD player, and when he turned back he found Mattie with her knees pulled to her chest, her hands covering her mouth as she listened. "You okay?" he asked.

She was quiet until the last notes faded away, leaving the room in silence. He thought that she might be ready to burst into tears again and he prepared himself for it, spying a new box of tissues that had been set on the piano. But before he could grab it she said, "You know, you may be right after all." Standing up scattered the array of tissues around her and unceremoniously dumped Max onto the floor. "Let's go running."

Chapter 30

Dear El,

I have just caused the mother of all bad situations. And all it would have taken was a single, solitary decision on my part to avoid it all.

After Graham and I parted company, I was a miserable bitch. Zack was trying just about anything to get me back to normal. His solution was to finally get me to form the dance hall band I'd been talking about for a year. So I ran auditions and saw half a dozen pianists. And then, who should walk in but Rhonda Harper. I knew exactly who she was-as soon as I saw the form she'd filled out. She was a pretty fair player, definitely the best of the bunch. And just for a second, I thought that I could not pick her for the job and avoid all kinds of hassles in the future. But no...I had to convince myself that I was a better person than that, and that I might as well try her and see how things worked out. Besides, I already had all the other musicians lined up. So I decided to give her a chance.

Well now Zack and Rhonda are the hot item in our social circle. And I'm finding that despite myself and every hateful impulse I've ever had, I'm beginning to like her. She's still seeing

Graham because she's providing music for the play he's doing. But she's just head over heels in love with Zack. And since he's my friend, I really don't have any alternative but to spend time with her.

The more I watch her with Zack though, the more I have to shake my head. Rhonda is very obviously one of those women that cannot function without a man in her life.

Mattie shook her head and scratched out the last line. She had to think about the emotionally correct way to phrase what she was trying to say.

The more I watch her with Zack though, the more I have to shake my head. Rhonda is very obviously one of those women that cannot function without a man in her life.

She can't seem to understand how any woman in her right mind can function as a complete person without being married. It seems to me that getting married is the end all and be all of her existence. She's only been dating Zack for a couple of months and they're already making wedding plans. And what's worse, she's taken to setting me up on blind dates.

God help me.

Zack and Mattie sat in a booth at a Whyte Avenue pub, with their respective dates at their sides. Rhonda was snuggled in against Zack just as tightly as she could be, while Mattie's date Alex sat at as discreet a distance as the booth allowed. Alex was a friend of Zack's from work, who had been lured by Rhonda to come along with the promise of a free movie ticket. Together the four of them were discussing the outcome of the foreign film they had all just been to see.

"You see," Alex pointed out, "this is what happens when a man dresses like a girl."

"You only say that because you wished it happened to you when we caught you wearing women's clothing," Zack reminded him.

Mattie laughed. "They caught you wearing a dress?"

"It was for Halloween!" Alex defended.

"Well, I think it's the best foreign movie I've ever seen," Mattie concluded. "It beats the hell out of that Spanish movie I keep seeing on TV – the one where the woman's two lovers beat each other to death with frozen ham hocks."

Rhonda added, "You know, I think I've seen that one." There was a laugh all around the table. It was broken by Rhonda, who was staring wide-eyed at the pub's main entrance. "Oh my god," she gasped.

All eyes followed her gaze, and all but Alex were astounded by what they saw.

"You have got to be kidding me," Mattie groaned.

All Zack could say was, "Christ."

Graham stood in the doorway, drawn up pompously tall and insufferable. Beside him was a very young woman, wearing a cut off tee-shirt and her dyed blonde hair tied in pigtails. She was latched onto Graham like a puppy, and together they made their way through the maze of tables to where the double date was sitting. "Well hi there," Graham greeted cheerfully. Then to Rhonda he said, "We thought we'd just drop in and see if you were here."

"You know I'm here almost every night," Rhonda reminded him, eyeing him skeptically.

Graham indicated his companion. "This is Teri."

In no mood for chitchat, Mattie took the forthright approach. "You don't have my big band anthology, do you?"

"No." Graham addressed the entire table again. "Well, we're going to get a drink. Just wanted to say hi." Teri gave everyone a little wave, and the couple turned to take a place at the bar. They left everyone gaping at them across the few feet that separated the two groups.

"Do you believe that?" Rhonda commented.

"How old is she, anyway?" Zack added.

Mattie regarded the young girl. "She can't be more than twenty-four."

Alex asked, "And how old is he?"

"A lot older than that."

There was a pause as everyone stopped to consider what they had just witnessed. Then Rhonda had a sudden inspiration. To Alex and Mattie she said, "I think you two should start making out."

Mattie frowned at her across the table. "What?"

"To make him jealous," Rhonda explained.

Mattie gave a sideways glance at Alex before telling Zack's girlfriend, "You're not helping!"

The main reason that Graham had come into the pub that night was to show his new girlfriend off to Rhonda, and to prove that she had chosen the wrong man. But she's so oblivious because of Zack that she had no clue what he was up to. I really felt sorry for Alex though - she put him under so much pressure on our double date that I never heard from him again.

"Helen!"

Helen's eyes squeezed tight shut, preparing her ears for another onslaught of Katrina's howling. The book in her hand closed with a sharp snap, skidding completely off the end of the coffee table when she tossed it down. She jumped to her feet and raced around the corner to the door to cut off her husband before he could holler for her again. "Keep your voice down!" she hissed before she even saw him. "Katrina is finally asleep!" He fixed her with a glare, one that made her stop in her tracks just by the entrance to the kitchen. "What?"

He pushed his way past her without another word and went into the living room. By the time she got there, he had collapsed down onto the couch where she had just been. Kevin let her stand there, staring at him for a minute or two before telling her, "Get me a beer."

Normally she would protest, but with the mood that he had been in for the last week, Helen decided that it was easier just to go to the fridge and retrieve a can. Once it was in his hand, she sat down beside him and asked again, "What's wrong?"

Kevin took a long swallow from the can, his eyes watering from the carbonation. He took his time, downing more than half the can before feeling like he could speak. "I got laid off."

Helen sat back, stunned. It was the first she had heard anything about it. And though it had been years since she stopped working to care for their kids, even she knew that there were always rumblings of impending doom when something like this was happening to a company. "What?" she gasped, unable to move.

"I said I got laid off!" He turned on her. "What part of that didn't you understand?"

"What are you yelling at me for?" she snapped, suddenly feeling defensive. "You haven't said anything about this before – how the hell do you expect me to react?"

Kevin jumped to his feet. "Well I would have hoped that my own wife would have been supportive. Or at least that she would feel sorry for me!"

"Don't talk about me like I'm not here!" She stood up, pulling herself up into her full height as she glared at him.

"Why not? It seems to me that you're never here anyway."

Helen was taken aback. "What the hell does that mean?"

His eyes rolled. "It means I expect to find you here when I get home at night."

"Does that mean I'm not supposed to have a life of my own?" she challenged.

"I didn't say that."

"Only what?" Helen had felt this fight coming for some time now, and this seemed as good a time as any. "You're bitching about the one day you actually came home straight after work? The rest of the time you're never home before ten o'clock anyway. Of course I'm going to be home by then!" She started to pace the width of the living room, careful not to close any of the distance between them.

"So I don't get home before ten," he countered. "So what?"

"You haven't seen your kids in more than a week," she reminded him, her voice turning into a low growl.

"I've been busting my ass to make sure that this family is fed." As soon as he said it, the full realization of his new work situation hit him. He had no job. The only person in the family that worked, he was supposed to pay for their food and their new townhouse. For clothes and entertainment. "Oh Jesus," he mumbled, sinking down into the worn armchair in the corner and burying his face in his hands.

The black cloud over Helen broke, and her heart was flooded with sympathy. She knelt down at the arm of the chair, resting her hands on his knee as she spoke softly. "We're going to get through this, Kevin. We'll ride it out."

He didn't respond, and was frighteningly still. "Are you listening to me?" she asked, careful to ensure that the question did not sound like an accusation.

"Leave me alone," he warned, pushing her hands off.

"Kevin…"

"I said leave me alone!" In a flash his arm struck out to shove her away, so hard that she tumbled back into the edge of the nearby dining room table. A sickening thud filled the room when her head hit the top before she collapsed down hard onto the floor. He didn't move from the chair, just glaring at her as she tried to cover up the pain with her fingers.

In the background she could hear the baby starting to cry again, as well as her older brother calling out in fright, though the sounds barely penetrated the waves of pain that were radiating through her head. It had all happened so fast that it took her a moment to realize she was on the floor, and that Kevin was still watching her from the same place that he had struck her. She froze in fear, not knowing what to do next. He had never hit her before.

Kevin slowly got up, seeing her shrink back from him as he approached her. All he said to her was, "Why can't you ever listen?" He walked over to retrieve his keys, then silently walked out the door.

Chapter 31

Graham left his doctor's office and headed for the bank of elevators that ran down the center of the building. After a longer than usual wait, the down arrow above him flashed red, and the doors slid open to admit him. He punched the button for the main floor, then leaned back into the corner to take some of the pressure off his feet. *He's right,* he told himself when he thought about his doctor's most recent advice. *I really do need to lose some weight.*

All thoughts about his medical problems disappeared when the elevator slowed and stopped a mere three floors below where he had started. A raven-haired woman stepped inside, immediately moving to the opposite side of the small chamber when she saw that the correct button had already been pushed. She did the same as he did and leaned back into the opposite corner as she watched the floors count down.

When they passed the fifth floor, both staggered forward when the elevator car lurched and then dropped to a sudden halt. Since Graham was closest to the control panel, he started punching a variety of buttons to try and get them moving. When nothing worked, he finally reached down and pulled open the compartment that contained the emergency phone. The person who answered told him that a repair crew was on its way, and he relayed the information to the other passenger as he hung up.

"Oh this is just great," she complained as she checked her watch. Next she dug around her purse, but came up short. "Excuse me," she said as she turned to Graham. "Do you happen to have a cell phone with you?"

"Yeah, sure." He reached around to grab it from where it was kept on his belt, then handed it to her. "Here you go."

"Thanks." She quickly examined the face to familiarize herself, started punching buttons, then stopped and handed it back to him. "It's dead."

Graham checked everything, then muttered, "Oh shit," when he saw that she was right. "I'm sorry," he apologized as he replaced it on his belt. "I must have forgotten to lock it and accidentally dialed someone."

"That's alright," she shrugged, retreating back into the corner. "I'm already running late." She checked her watch again. "Did they say how long it's going to be?"

"No."

She folded her arms across her chest and rested one ankle over the other when she sat down on the floor. To herself she grumbled, "Like I really needed to give my mother more ammunition."

"I take it you're going to see her," Graham said as he sat down in his own corner.

She nodded. "I'm supposed to be taking her to her sister's tonight. I thought we were just going to be late, but now it looks like we're not going to get there at all."

The two of them fell silent for the next half hour, with her reading through the papers that she had been carrying. He spent his time trying not to stare at her too much.

She was younger than he was. But then, he reminded himself, these days it seemed like everybody was. And since he made it a habit to hang out with people younger than him, it had turned into something of an occupational hazard. She was small in most every way, from her build to her haircut, and he couldn't help but be fascinated. "Can I ask you something?" he finally ventured.

"What's that?" she responded, briefly glancing up from the papers in her hand.

"You single?"

She wasn't sure. Her life was such a mess at the moment, she didn't know where to start. Looking him over, the first thing she noticed was that he had a kind face, which smiled pleasantly at her as he patiently waited for her answer. "I am," she said softly, the beginnings of a smile forming at the corner of her mouth.

He nodded, taking in that bit of information. "So...could I interest you in coffee?" he asked. "I mean when you're not late for meeting your mother or stuck in an elevator or something."

The young woman laughed. "I think I could be convinced."

"Good." He crawled over and extended his hand. "My name's Graham."

"Giorgina."

Three months later, Mattie was asked by a friend to sing at his wedding, as a surprise for his bride. She was more than happy to accept, and since Zack was invited as well, she asked Rhonda to play piano for her. During Mattie's discussions with the groom, she found out that Graham had managed to bully his way into an invitation and made the mistake of telling Rhonda. With her own relationship running along smoothly, Rhonda immediately started conjuring dozens of scenarios to embarrass Graham and make him feel as tall as an ant.

Mattie asked her friend Nathan to go along on the road trip as her date, and he graciously accepted her invitation. They had known each other for years, but had only recently begun spending time together. Always one to jump at an opportunity to set Mattie up, Rhonda had decided that the two of them would make an ideal couple and had been forcing the issue the moment the invitations were received. Mattie asked her to back off the subject repeatedly, quickly becoming infuriated when her pleas fell on deaf ears. Whether it was intentional or not, what Rhonda had thought amusing was a prominent embarrassment to both Mattie and Nathan. Even Zack, who was still buried deep under his blinded love, had managed to get up enough nerve to say a few words to his girlfriend. She let the subject drop, without really ever knowing that she had been maneuvered into it.

The four of them actually looked forward to the road trip for months, once things settled down. Mattie couldn't tell how Nathan felt about it, but she was grateful for the fact that he hadn't backed out after all the pressuring from Rhonda.

They arrived at the hotel early on Saturday afternoon, which was a couple blocks away from the church. It took only half an hour to get ready and then, with the guys in their suits and the girls wearing gowns, they walked over for the ceremony. Decked out in sunglasses, they were the epitome of cool, young adulthood.

They kept themselves occupied as they walked, talking excitedly between one another. They were still a good distance from the church when they spotted Graham leaning up against his car, smoking a cigarette. Mattie saw him first. "God give me strength," she muttered under her breath. Nathan rested a hand on her back to comfort her a little, happy to see her smile at him in return.

"You know," Rhonda said, "I was kind of hoping that he wouldn't show up."

"Then you'd have moped all night because you wouldn't have had anyone to make fun of," Zack told her. Rhonda slapped him lightly across the shoulder, then linked her arm with his so that there would be no mistaking who she was there with.

Looking ahead, they could see an unfamiliar woman standing next to him, tall and curvy, dressed in a conservative suit. Leaving that puzzle aside for the moment, they tried to get past him and into the church. But Graham cheerfully greeted, "Hi there," before they could get inside.

They all, with the exception of Mattie, said hello to the unwanted wedding guest. There was only a tiny bit of idle chitchat before the younger group went into the church, laughing at Graham and speculating over his new girlfriend all the way to their seats.

When it was time for the newlyweds to sign the register, Mattie and Rhonda made their way up to the piano to deliver the surprise that the groom had successfully arranged for his bride. Mattie faced the congregation and as she sang, she found her eyes flitting from one person to the next to see how they were reacting. Though she tried her best, her attention eventually and inevitably fell on Graham. It had been a long time since she had caught him listening to her sing in their apartment, and she was a little dismayed when she found that he was just simply watching her, very careful not to convey any kind of emotion. In the back of her mind, she had kind of hoped she would be able to captivate him like she had before.

The group was late in arriving to the dinner, after having a few drinks in their hotel room to waste time after the ceremony. Rhonda had flipped through the local phone book in order to look up an old friend, and curiosity got the better of Mattie. The book contained listings for all the local communities, including Valleyview. And sure enough, there was a listing for K. Delamont there, making her heart flutter for a beat. Here she was, close enough that she wouldn't even have to pay for the call. But then she started wondering what she would say, and also what would be said to her after years of separation. So she closed the book, and told Zack that she had found Helen. Then they headed off to the reception.

Rhonda was the first to spot Graham or, more accurately, he was the first one to spot them. He waved at her from across the hall, indicating that he had saved places for all of them to sit. Their solution was to go find a place of their own on the other side of the hall. Mattie and Nathan sat with their backs to that direction, and Rhonda had mercifully been able to stay off the topic. They made it through dinner, and then it was on to the dance.

The emcee called for the new couple to head into the middle of the floor, and then after each song ended, he would invite more people until the floor was filled with a variety of guests. Zack and Rhonda got up, their arms wrapped around each other's waist until they found a small clearing to move within. Nathan stood up and offered his hand to Mattie, patiently waiting for her to put down her drink and join him in a dance.

Despite everyone's intentions, Mattie was still preoccupied with the man on the other side of the room. As they danced, Nathan couldn't help but notice that her eyes never left him, and were watching every move that he made. "You know," he said, trying to get her attention, "you sang really great today."

"Thanks," she replied automatically, not actually hearing what he had said. She was watching as Graham tried to navigate the dance floor, and it was painfully obvious that he and his new girlfriend had never danced together before. It was also obvious that they were not the lovers that he tried to make them appear to be.

Seeing that he hadn't reached her, Nathan tried to get her attention again. "I think that your voice is really developing," he complimented. "You sound a lot better than you did a few months ago."

This time she actually did hear him, and when she finally saw him she mentally kicked herself. Nathan was as nice and understanding a friend as she could have asked for; he listened to her complain incessantly about being subjected to Zack and Rhonda's public displays and about Rhonda's obsession with her single status, but never said a negative word about it. He was handsome, talented, and was starting to slowly develop an interest in her – one that she was too lovesick and angry to see. "I'm sorry," she whispered, her cheeks reddening a little as she looked at the floor.

Nathan spun her around so that her back was to her ex-best friend. "It's okay," he assured her, throwing a little more effort into his dance steps. "It sucks, doesn't it?"

Zack and Rhonda fell into her line of sight as soon as Nathan turned her, and seeing them making out on the dance floor was just another knife in her heart. She closed her eyes tight, trying to drive the images from her mind. When they opened again, Nathan was the first thing she saw. "I hope you don't think I brought you here as a security blanket," she said, barely loud enough for him to hear over the music.

He shook his head. "I never thought that." But her attention inevitably wandered again, so rather than continue to torture her he offered, "Come on – let me buy you a drink."

Later on in the evening, Mattie had managed to achieve her goal of tying one on – the four of them managing to put away more than their fair share of liquor. Mattie's worries disappeared more with every glass until she no longer dwelled on Graham – she had forgotten that he was there at all.

At around midnight, Mattie headed for her drink when a long stretch of line dancing had turned her knees to jelly. Rhonda was at the table, taking a moment to fan herself with a folded up program from the church. "Wow," Mattie gasped after downing the last of her drink. "I have to go outside and cool off."

"Maybe you shouldn't go out there," Rhonda advised.

Mattie, who had crouched down to retrieve her purse from under the table, stuck her head back up over the white tablecloth. "Why not?"

"Because the guys are out there."

Mattie stood back up, an eyebrow lifting in interest. "So?"

"Well…they're talking about guy stuff."

"Guy stuff?" Mattie shook her head at Rhonda's odd reason and announced, "Please – I invented guy stuff." Then she headed outside to find Nathan and Zack, just as Rhonda had warned her.

"Yeah, I would," Zack told Nathan.

"Would what?" she questioned, coming up between them as she fished her cigarettes out of her purse.

They weren't at all embarrassed at being caught, so Nathan told her, "We were talking about the women here that we would sleep with."

"Which one?"

"The one in the green dress." Nathan nodded toward the tall, dark-haired woman near the door who was decked in a form-fitting Lycra dress that reminded Mattie of a Jell-O mold.

The lighter in Mattie's hand clicked when she let go of the button, and she took a good look at the woman as she blew out her first puff of smoke. "I'd convert," she finally announced, making the other two laugh. But her laughter was cut short when she saw Graham walk outside to satisfy his own nicotine craving. He also saw them, and so he stayed within a few feet of the door, falling back against the concrete wall and letting his eyes slide shut as he smoked.

The guys both turned to see what she was staring at. Zack warned, "Mattie – don't."

She swaggered through the gap between them, assuring them both, "I'm not going to do anything," as she went by. The cigarette was sent flying across the parking lot with a flick of her fingers, followed by slow, deliberate steps as she walked up to face him. Sensing that someone was in front of him, Graham opened his eyes to see Mattie, her arms folded across her chest, eyes blazing with defiance. "What are you doing here?" she growled.

"I was invited," he said coldly.

"What do you do," she questioned, "follow me around?" Out of the corner of her eye, she could see Zack and Nathan approaching. They wanted to be there just in case things got out of hand.

Graham glanced at the approaching pair, also aware of their purpose there. Doing his best to maintain his temper, his tones were very measured when he challenged, "What are you talking about?"

"Why are you there every time I turn around?" she accused. "Can't you take a fucking hint?"

"Matt, come on," Nathan tried to persuade her, gently taking her arm by the elbow.

She wrenched herself out of his grip and continued on her tirade. "Don't you realize you're not wanted here?"

Now any maintenance of his temper was rapidly disappearing. A low growl emanated from the back of Graham's throat, and once again Nathan tried to pull Mattie away. "Let me go!" she snapped at him. "Well?" she directed back at Graham.

"Shut up, Mattie," he warned.

But once started, she was not about to stop. "Or what?" she taunted. "You gonna hit me?"

"Mattie…" Zack tried again.

"I would never hit you," he snarled back.

"Oh really?" Before anyone, not even Mattie, realized what she was doing she slugged him, her knuckles landing in his left temple with enough force to spin him up against the wall. Zack and Nathan moved in to pull her away, and it took both of them to keep her from going after her target again. "Let me go!" she shouted at them. Then to Graham she hollered, "Leave me alone, you son of a bitch!" The guys actually had her up off her feet, and she continued to try to get them to drop her. "Put me down!"

"Maybe you'd better take her back to the hotel," Zack suggested as they hauled her to the other side of the parking lot.

"Good idea," Nathan agreed. They put her back down on her feet when they reached the sidewalk, both maintaining a firm grip on her when she tried to bolt again. "Come on," he ordered. "We're going for a walk."

"I don't want to go for a walk!" she protested.

"You need to cool off," he insisted, reaching for her shoulders to turn her in the direction of the hotel.

She looked back over her shoulder as Nathan led her away, still spitting curses under her breath while pain started to radiate through the knuckles in her right hand. Nathan kept a firm hand on her until the reception hall was well out of sight, and he couldn't help but shake his head. Even though she was drunk, he never would have guessed that she would have laid Graham out.

Mattie continued to curse, stomping her way down the street until they reached a park bench that was bolted to the corner. There were a few feet separating her from her friend, so it took a few seconds for him to catch up when she flopped down onto it. Her eyes peered up at him from under lowered brows, and as she regarded him she asked, "What is it with you guys?"

"What do you mean?" he countered, thinking better of his impulse to sit down next to her.

"Why do you all have to lie to me? Why do you all have to wait for years to get to know me before you decide you want to be more than my friend? And then you all of a sudden decide that I wasn't what you really wanted after all." Mattie stared at him for a moment, and when he didn't answer she turned away from him. She didn't dare show him the tears that were forming in her eyes.

He finally opted to sit next to her, but at a discreet distance. "We're not all like Graham and Zack, you know." Her small, huffed laugh gave him the confidence to press on. "Some of us even have some honor." Nathan swallowed hard, wondering why he couldn't summon up the nerve to comfort her like he wanted to. Though he didn't realize it, deep down inside he knew that she was in no condition to consider him, and he was not interested in being her rebound. So he buried his feelings down deep, and simply rested a hand on her shoulder to show his support.

The next morning, Mattie found herself alone in their hotel room when Zack and Rhonda went out for a walk and Nathan had started packing the car. She was moving slowly, trying to avoid exacerbating her headache as she put her clothes into her knapsack. Her eyes were barely opened, so she didn't see the nightstand when she turned around, and her bruised knuckles hit it with a loud bang. She cursed loudly, clutching the wound to her chest and reeling at the sound of her own voice ringing in her ears.

Nathan came back into the room, pouring sunlight into the far corner. He wore a pleasant smile on his face and greeted, "Good morning."

"Morning," she grumbled, gingerly rubbing the pain from her knuckles.

"How are you doing?"

She slowly sat down, resignation filling her voice. "My head feels like the ball in a World Cup match."

"I can understand that," he empathized, stepping toward the windows. "I never would have bet you could make Zack drink that much." He threw the curtains open, flooding the room with light. Mattie groaned, fell over onto the mattress and hid her eyes behind her fingers to avoid being blinded. Nathan turned around, then grabbed the sunglasses off his head and tossed them to her. "Here. These will help."

Her hangover fully controlled the speed at which she was doing anything, but she did manage to put the sunglasses on before taking a look at him. He was showered, fully groomed and wearing a pleasant expression as he sat down in front of her on the opposite bed. She fixed him with a look, her brow furrowed. "Why are you so happy?"

"It's morning," he replied.

Behind the dark blue lenses, her eyes rolled. "Oh give me a break, will you." To complete her display of dissatisfaction, she rolled over onto her back and laid her forearm over his glasses.

Nathan leaned forward, resting his elbows on his knees when he told her, "You know, you were something last night."

Panic gripped her heart – try as she might, she barely remembered a few details of the night before. "What do you mean?" she questioned warily, not really sure that she wanted to hear the answer.

"I mean at the party. You were so worried about being around Zack and Rhonda for an evening. But it didn't seem to bother you."

"If you drank as much as I did," she reminded him, "you wouldn't care either."

There was a balled up pair of socks on the bed near her pillow, and he absently picked them up and started rolling them between his palms. "No, I mean it. From the moment you started singing, the place was yours."

Mattie finally lifted her arm to peer at him with an unbelieving stare. "I think you're forgetting the bride and groom."

"There was a bride and groom?"

"Look," she told him as she slowly sat up, "I appreciate you trying to boost my ego. But all I want is to be left alone to wallow in my own misery."

He was stunned, and a little hurt by her rejection of his attempt to make her feel better. "Okay...if that's what you want." He got up and headed for the door, telling her on his way out, "Come on, they're waiting for us."

Mattie didn't really notice that she had inflicted any pain on him, but was instead concentrating on pulling herself together and moving with some pride when she headed out the door. A groan was ripped from her when the sun hit her in full force, but she shut the door and caught up with Nathan as he made his way down the outdoor stairs. Rhonda and Zack were already waiting at the car, rearranging the packing that Nathan had done a few minutes before. "Did you guys decide where we're going for breakfast?" Mattie asked them as she threw her stuff in the back.

"We figured we'd go back to the same place we went yesterday," Nathan told her as he reached in to rearrange her luggage. "Seems as good as anything."

Zack's car was parked in front of one of the rooms on the motel's lower level, and at that moment the door opened. The group around the car froze in silence. Graham was standing there, his hand on the doorknob as he talked to Giorgina. He too froze when he saw them, none of them knowing what to say. The area around his left eye was heavy with blue and purple, and to Mattie he looked like he'd had the roughest of nights.

Nathan glanced at Mattie, and he couldn't help but grin. He leaned over to her and whispered, "Oh by the way, you decked Graham last night."

She continued to stare at her adversary, and did not whisper when she questioned, "When did I do that?"

Now Nathan was on the verge of laughter. "On the way back here."

Mattie couldn't help but smirk, her eyes never leaving Graham. "I did a good job, didn't I?"

"Yeah, you could say that." Nathan laid a hand on her shoulder to tell her it was time to go, before anything else could happen.

Rhonda was holding the passenger door open, and just before she ducked inside Mattie told the unwelcome guest, "You must have really pissed somebody off last night." She then climbed inside, leaving Graham to gape at them, wordless until long after their car pulled away.

Chapter 32

A rain-filled Saturday threatened to pull Mattie into a tailspin. It was a day incredibly similar to the one that had put her under the bridge with Graham a year before. So she took a long bath, blasted some music and called on her friends for a night out. Usually when Mattie called her friends for a martini night, a group of at least a dozen would invade a Whyte Avenue bar. But this time, it only ended up being Mattie, Nathan, Rhonda and Zack. The relationship between Mattie and Nathan had become strained, though she really wasn't sure why. Rhonda had tried to tell her that it was because he loved her, but Mattie didn't believe her – she wasn't about to fall into that trap again. But even though the pair seemed to be at odds, they still got along quite well in large groups.

Zack had left to pick his mother up from the airport, with a promise to return soon. About half an hour later, Mattie recognized Nathan's best friend Josh walk into the bar. "Hey man," he greeted when he reached the table, "you ready to go?"

"Just about," the other replied, reaching for his wallet.

"Where are you going?" Mattie questioned.

"To the movies." He picked a couple of bills and tossed them down onto the table. "Wanna come?"

She checked her watch, noticing that it had gotten pretty late. "Nah. I'm not into a movie tonight." Her eyes flicked over to the empty chair across the way. "Besides, somebody's got to keep Rhonda company till Zack comes back."

"Okay. See you later." He jumped up and disappeared, leaving the two women behind.

Rhonda watched them until they were out of sight, while Mattie turned her attention back to the remaining fries on her plate. Her companion suddenly said, "You've pretty much given up on him, haven't you?"

Mattie had grown weary of revisiting this topic time and time again. No matter how much she tried, she could never convince Zack's girlfriend that she had absolutely no interest in Nathan. Or at least that she refused to allow herself to be interested. So in an attempt to sidestep the issue she simply responded, "Pretty much."

Any hope of a peaceful end to the discussion vanished with, "He's kind of immature, huh?"

Mattie disagreed wholeheartedly, but she really didn't want to discuss the matter. "Uh huh."

"So you keep looking somewhere else."

Mattie turned her attention out to the rest of the pub, trying to remain neutral. "I don't feel like looking anymore."

Rhonda regarded the other woman, giving them a moment of relative silence. "You still have feelings for Graham, don't you?"

Mattie whirled on her, fire flashing in her eyes as a sudden wave of anger pulsed through her body. Ever mindful of appearances, she held a tight control over her voice when she growled, "I hate him. I don't have any feelings for that man."

Rhonda continued undaunted. "Well let's face facts – usually if you hate somebody that much, it's because you've felt extremely close to them in the past."

"That is such bullshit. I just hate him. That's all."

Rhonda shrugged. "We'll just have to find you a new one."

Mattie's eyes rolled as she turned back to look into the crowded bar. A sigh of relief escaped her when she saw Zack come in. Maybe he would distract his girlfriend from her line of conversation. "You're back," she announced, a slight smile on her lips and desperation on her face.

He walked right past Mattie and bent down to kiss his girlfriend in greeting. "You owe me six bucks," Rhonda told him.

"For what?" He dropped down into the chair beside her.

"You left without paying."

"Oh, I'm sorry." He had adopted the silly, lilting voice that he saved only for Rhonda, and Mattie turned away as the couple began to shower each other with kisses.

When they finally broke apart, Rhonda told Mattie, "You should come to my office barbecue."

Looking skeptical and uninterested, Mattie knew she would regret asking, "What for?"

Rhonda lit up with the prospect of making a match. "We've got this great guy at work – the marketing director. He's cute and funny, and he's got loads of earning potential."

"And he'll probably go running in the other direction when he sees me coming," Mattie shot out, now looking for whatever would stop this inquisition.

Rhonda leaned back against the arm that Zack had put around her shoulders, her head cocked to the side as she regarded their companion. "Now what kind of attitude is that?"

"A truthful one."

"Don't be so bitter."

For some reason Mattie was unable to get up and leave, despite every impulse she felt to flee. In a deep, carefully controlled voice she growled, "I *like* being bitter."

As she turned away, Rhonda pressed, "Well maybe being bitter is the reason you can't find a man."

"What are you, my mother?"

"Well *I* think it's true."

Mattie turned back on her vehemently "Look...I have every right to be bitter. Any man I take an interest in is always one of three things – they like me only as the funny fat girl, they 'just aren't interested in dating anyone right now', or they seem to think that I'm one half of their 'matched woman' set. Everything is perfect as long as he's allowed to have a wife and something on the side."

"Well I've dated those," Rhonda countered, the slightest frown creeping between her eyebrows.

Mattie stared at her for a second, unable to believe that the tirade she had just laid out failed to stop this ridiculous conversation. Filled with resignation, she sighed, "Apparently I'm destined to date nothing but assholes."

"Yeah, well I've dated a lot of those too."

The subject of her criticism narrowed her eyes. "Look, I'm just a lucky charm for men." At this point, she was willing to do just about anything to get Rhonda off her back. "Once they stop dating me, they all find these wonderful relationships."

"Well you sure took your time with me," Zack interjected suddenly.

Mattie tried to kill him with her eyes. "I'm sorry...did I not have my life torn apart soon enough for your liking?"

He was backpedalling as soon as he saw the look, and sheepishly apologized, "Sorry."

"You two are driving me crazy," Mattie muttered as she sank back into her seat.

"We aren't that bad," he tried to point out.

"Really? You know, when Nathan yells at you to get a room, he's not kidding." Then she turned her focus back to Rhonda. "I have sat here and watched him treat you better than he ever treated me when we were dating."

"So what?" Now there was finally a reaction, realization in Rhonda that this was not a one-sided lecture for Mattie's benefit. She suddenly went on the defensive. "I've waited a long time for this."

"Oh get over yourself!" Mattie shot back. "Just because you're dating somebody doesn't mean that everybody else has to be too."

"I never said..."

She was on a roll, and was not about to be interrupted. "Who just told me that I have come to her staff barbecue to meet the single guy? I never had any interest in Nathan, and yet you felt the need to push that on him until he felt so uncomfortable that he hates being around me." In the split second it took to draw breath, she suddenly realized that she had found a possible explanation for the tension. But that could wait until later. "I don't have to sit here and defend myself to you because I don't have a date. It's bad enough that you're the reason Graham and I never got together, but I will not sit here and let you insult me. You have done nothing but push on this since the day I met you, and the only reason you're so gung-ho about it is that you're scared that I'm going to take Zack off into the nearest corner and fuck him as soon as you're out of earshot." She leaned across the table to get into Rhonda's face. "Now maybe somebody like you can't understand this, but if I want to be bitter and lonely that's my business!" She stormed out of the pub, leaving the stunned pair in silence.

The skies had opened and it was raining, but she didn't notice. Adrenaline was coursing through her, and Mattie vaguely noticed the people that darted around her as they tried to find shelter from the downpour. She replayed the past few minutes in her mind, and then started to wander the busy street in a direction opposite from where she'd parked her car. Tears streamed down her face, conveniently hidden by the rain.

It was then that I realized that I had never been allowed to cry. All the times that friends and family had cut phone calls short, or struggled to find an excuse to change the subject...it all suddenly made sense. Rhonda and Zack were nauseatingly in love, and it seemed that as long as you were in love, no one forced you to stop showing it. But when things have gone wrong and you feel absolutely pathetic, no one wants to be around you.

I had listened to Rhonda in earnest ever since I hired her, desperately seeking a replacement for all the best friends I've lost over the last three years. I was so desperate for a friend that I let her push me far away from the person that I am. And I was so desperate to try to regain the ground I was losing in my depression that I was willing to listen to and ally myself with almost anybody.

Rhonda and Zack formally announced their engagement about a month after that, and they got married the following May – a year after they first met. Zack and I spoke only sporadically during that time, and I have never felt so disregarded in my life. It was quite clear that Rhonda had forbidden him from spending any time with me, and I suddenly discovered that he didn't have the balls to stand up to her like I thought he would. One night he tried to make me feel better when he came over with my invitation to their wedding, telling me that he had fought a round with his mother-in-law in order to secure it. Apparently she has the same ex-girlfriend paranoia as her daughter. I told him to stick it – that he wasn't doing me any favors, and then I bawled that night because I felt so victimized by the whole situation. Everybody seemed to conveniently forget that if it hadn't been for me, those two never would have met in the first place.

I also heard that Graham rolled his car around that time, and my spies told me that he spent about a month in the hospital. Part of me wanted to run to him, to make sure he was okay and to forgive all past transgressions. But the stubborn side of me, for once, wouldn't allow it – the part that finally woke up and realized that he isn't any good for me. I comforted myself with the thought that he would already have somebody there to take care of him, not to mention the fact that despite all of her ranting and raving, Rhonda had decided to be friends with him again. The last thing I could have handled was accidentally running into them at the hospital.

The worst part of it all was the depression. Nearly two years' worth. Two years of days filled with such bone-chilling loneliness that there's nothing you can do but stare out a window and cry. I can't remember how many times I did that – wept openly and unabashedly with the kind of tears I've never let anyone see. I felt so sorry for myself because I seemed to have lost most of the things that had filled my life. I've always considered my closest friends to be family – you know that. But I also felt guilty – so guilty for indulging in the self-pity. There are people in this world who have lost so much more, and they managed to have reclaimed their lives.

I suddenly woke up one day and discovered that I was two years older, and that nothing had been accomplished with my life. All I could do was relive what happened with Graham, and wallow in how betrayed I felt when his love turned out to only be for convenience. And with you, I agonized over the loss of my soul mate – my sister. And then to have Zack – the one who promised to help me when I felt the lowest – turn his back on me in pursuit of his cock... It was all too much.

I can still feel it pulling at me, but now it seems much easier to work around. I have to make a conscious effort to keep positive, and it's starting to pay off. I feel better, am healthier than I have ever been in my life, and I'm starting to feel the need to get out and socialize with people again. I never stopped working, but when I listen to the recordings I did in that time, it's really easy to see that there was no soul there.

I feel restless now, unhappy about the grass that's grown under my feet. So I've finally decided to make the break for the coast and start over again.

There's just one person I have to see first.

A knock on the plain wooden door prompted Graham to slowly get up from the couch. He squinted through the peep hole, stood back and cocked his head, then took another look to make sure. It took a moment or two for him to deliberate, but he finally opened the door.

Standing in the hallway was someone that he had desperately wished to see for the last two years. A slim and quite nervous Mattie Forrest suddenly looked up from the doorknob that she had been unconsciously staring at while she waited. Surprised to find that he was home, for a second she stared at him as if he was the headlights to her deer. She quietly said, "This was a bad idea," and headed back toward the stairwell.

He let her get a few steps away before calling after her, "No wait!" When she turned around, Mattie saw that he had been reaching out after her, but as soon as she saw him his hand dropped. He offered, "Why don't you come in?"

Mattie thought about it for a few moments, her eyes examining the hallway around her. She knew the reason she came tonight – she had to tell him she was leaving. To end their relationship once and for all. But fear had seized her heart, and she wasn't sure of herself anymore. In Graham's eyes she could see the happiness her arrival had given him. So she drew a deep breath, pasted a smile on her face, and stepped into his apartment.

It was exactly as she remembered it, right down to its cluttered state. The ashtrays were spilling over, black soot collected around his computer screen. Mattie smiled to herself – Graham's cleaning habits had certainly not improved in the past couple of years.

Two years. The passage of time hit Graham hard, emphasized by how different she looked now. Her rounded face was gone, gently shaped below cheekbones that he had never noticed. Before he could catch himself he heaved a sigh, which prompted her to turn around. "Can I get you something?" he quickly covered, heading into the tiny kitchen.

"Just some water, thanks." She took time to examine a new piece of artwork on the east wall. Its subtle curves and watery colors soothed her a little, helping to calm the butterflies in her stomach. He appeared at her side with her glass almost instantly, then offered her a seat. She thanked him for the drink and took a place at the end of the couch.

Graham sat at the opposite end, not sure of how to proceed. There were a lot of things he wanted to tell her all at once, about what he'd been through and how much he missed her. Just her presence was stirring up old feelings in him. "So...how have you been?" he finally asked.

"I've been good." She took a sip of water, then set her glass down on the coffee table.

They fell into a distressed silence, neither one sure of what to say. One would catch the other looking at them, then quickly look away on the pretense of not being caught. It took a long time before either one ventured to speak, and when they did, they ended up talking at the same time. Both laughed, breaking the tension a little as they lapsed back into silence. Finally he said, "You look great."

Ever since she lost her extra weight, Mattie had to fight her automatic reaction of doubting the sincerity of the person complimenting her. So there was a pause while she reminded herself that it was okay for her to accept it. "Thanks." Reprogramming her mental script was, after all, the hardest part about becoming thin. Grasping for something to talk about, she ventured, "How's Giorgina?"

"Um..." The hands that he had placed in his lap now started fiddling and pulling at his fingers. "I haven't seen her in months."

There was something strange in the way that he said it. Mattie wondered whether or not she should even ask. But with nothing else to say she ventured, "I'm sorry."

"It was my own fault," he told her, suddenly full of truth. "I cheated on her."

For all his faults, infidelity was not usually one of them. "You cheated on her?"

"Uh huh." He sighed. "And I've paid for it." She must have silently questioned him because he added, "I got into a car accident on the way home that night."

"I heard about that." Mattie finally turned to face him. "I'm sorry I didn't come see you in the hospital."

Graham gave her a funny look – he had convinced himself that she hadn't known about the accident. It was the only explanation he was willing to accept for her never showing up at the hospital. And her inquiry now came just a little late. "I thought maybe you hadn't heard," he told her, hurt creeping into his voice.

She frowned, his attempt at guilt not lost on her. "I know." The comment weighed heavily on her, but she refused to let him transfer his remorse onto her. "Who was she?"

It caught him completely off guard, and Graham could feel some degree of contempt rise up in him because it really wasn't any of her business. It cooled in an instant and left him subdued, though still a little angry when he admitted, "One of her coworkers. I felt so awful about it that I wasn't paying attention to the road the night that Giorgina found out."

Unable to resist the opportunity, Mattie shot at him, "You should."

With that, he realized that they were falling back into the exact same pattern that they had been in so many times before, managing to pick up more or less where they had left off. "Believe me, I do." He smiled a little. "God, I've missed you."

"I've missed you too." She saw him twitch the slightest bit, encouraging her to follow her feelings and let him hug her. His presence was still very familiar to her, so Mattie had absolutely no problem melting in his arms. Her eyes slid shut, a silent sigh telling both of them that she had once again found the place she had always felt comfortable.

Graham could smell the apple-scented shampoo she had used on her short hair that morning, mixed together with the designer perfume that he had helped her pick out a few birthdays before. Her skin was soft and warm against his cheek, the edge of her earring digging slightly into his jaw. His pulse was pounding through his ears, so much that he was sure she would be able to hear it. He also closed his eyes, trying to will his heart to slow down and let him think calmly through the moment. As soon as she pulled away their eyes locked. Each looked deeply into the other's, seeking the one thing they hadn't been able to find in all the years that they'd known each other. But Mattie was leaving, and whether or not she found it tonight, it did not matter.

One moment they were in awkward silence, the next they were wrapped tightly in each other's arms. They kissed with a feverish pace, trying to make up for lost time. All of the memories of moments like this flooded back to both of them at once, and for a split second Graham considered breaking it off and asking her to leave. But he realized that there had to be a very good reason for her arrival at his apartment, so he decided that he was going to take the opportunity being presented to him now.

Mattie could feel him trying to push her onto her back, but she fought to remain upright, wanting to maintain control. In response Graham fell back, maintaining his grip and pulling her down on top of him. Her own heart was racing, her rapid breathing muffled by her close contact with him. They fell into the same rhythm that they always had together, keeping each other busy on the couch for only a few minutes before they paused. "If you're going to stop," she gasped, "you'd better do it now."

Graham answered by getting onto his feet and extending his hand out to her. Without hesitation she took it, snatching her purse up with the other hand and allowing him to pull her into his bedroom.

Her rasped breathing was stretched a little thinner when he lay down on top of her, but in light of what was happening it was something she was willing to live with. Graham did notice the strain it was putting on her, so he shifted off to one side to put her at ease. It also gave him a little more mobility, allowing him to start moving back to nibble at her ears. Mattie started to run her fingertips back and forth along the length of his back, one hand creeping around the side to run across the front. He grunted a huff of breath in response to her touch, and then decided that it was her turn.

Mattie fought her passions in order to keep her eyes open. She wanted to see everything that was happening now, to compare it to everything that she had imagined it would be. She had found that the dim lighting of a bedroom gave any man a soft, romantic look, and was delighted to know that Graham was no exception to that personal rule. He came up and kissed her again, his eyes popping open halfway through to gaze into hers. A glance down her body told her what he had in mind, so she pulled away to allow him to do his work.

Graham kissed his way down the front of her neck and stopped where the two sides of her blouse met. His fingers carefully separated each button, which was followed by a gentle kiss. The rest of the buttons were opened in the same way, and at last he was allowed to reveal her smooth, light skin. Her red underwire was dark in the limited street light that filtered in through the window, its satin molding shimmering. He kissed his way back up from the waist of her jeans, producing a sigh from her when he started to lick at the edge of the bra's fabric. He was taking his time, teasing her as he imagined he would if ever given the chance.

Mattie attempted to work her hands into the space between them, but her partner's long body made running her fingers across his chest out of reach. He pushed her arms up over her head, so she decided to settle back and enjoy herself for the moment. After a while he stopped and sat up, straddling her hips so that he could maneuver and hooking a finger underneath the bottom ridge of her bra. "Come here," he whispered as he laid his head down at the foot of the bed.

She did as he asked, crawling forward on all fours to reach him. As they kissed, she felt his hands run up her arms and over her shoulders. Her attention to him was enough to keep him from thinking clearly, which made combat with a bra catch trickier than usual. But his experienced hands took only a moment to free her.

They froze for just a moment, letting her breasts swing in the breeze that dusted in through the window. Then he took one onto his mouth and sent a whole new set of sensations rippling up into her back. A pang of fear struck in Mattie's stomach. They were breaking so many of the rules now, everything that both had wondered about since their romantic entanglement started. This had not been her intention when she came to visit him – she was going to tell him that she was leaving. When the tip of his tongue slid across to the other side, she allowed herself to get swept into the moment again. She would tell him. It would just be later.

Underneath her hips Mattie could feel him starting to grind against her, so she climbed down off of him and tugged him into an upright position. His shirt pulled out easily from under his belt, sliding up over his raised arms and popping off the top of his head as it mussed his hair. Mattie tossed the shirt down onto the floor, then leaned forward on her knees to start kissing him again. She loved the feel of bare skin against her own, which prompted her to pull him even tighter to her chest. He did the same, resulting in another explosion of tingles through both their bodies. Once again she ended up on her back, the air pushed out of her lungs when he fell on top of her.

Graham set to work on her chest again, taking great mouthfuls of flesh and holding them between his teeth so that his tongue could dance across them. A free hand toyed with whichever breast he was not occupied with, and he switched back and forth every couple of minutes. When he decided to finally kiss his way back down to the button on her jeans, he could feel her entire body tense. It was too soon. So he crawled forward again in order to kiss her.

In her own mind, Mattie remarked about the close call. She wanted him more than anything in the world, but fear of the unknown threatened to destroy the chance. Slow, deliberate progression was the best thing that they could possibly do now. He was flipped over onto his own back as she sat up, then proceeded to give him the same treatment that she had just received herself. Feeling a nipple underneath her tongue exhilarated Mattie, and she smiled by the reaction that he was having at her touch.

But Graham's patience was growing thin. He sat up, forcing her to sit back on her heels as he reached for the waistband of her jeans. Before she had a chance to think about it he had her pants and silky underwear down around her knees. Mattie stared down at her own body with a sudden attack of self-consciousness, and with a breath to steady herself, risked a look back up at him. His eyes were taking in every detail and memorizing the way that everything looked in the low light. He gasped, reaching out to wrap his hands around the back of her hips. "Come here."

"No," she tried to command. "Not now."

There was no derailing Graham's train of thought now, and he pulled her roughly up against his chest. "Yes now," he rasped in her ear. To cut off any possible argument from her, he started to lick at the curve of her ear and bit at the lobe. It worked, and he felt Mattie start to succumb to him. It wouldn't be long now.

Any thought of resistance that Mattie might have had was gone now, and while Graham rolled her down onto her back she kicked off what was left of her clothes. Her legs remained tightly together, and he teased her by brushing across her hips with the front of his jeans. "Oh god, I want you," she gasped, desperation entering her words. "Now?"

He stopped only long enough to look into her eyes and tell her, "Now would be good." While he was distracted by getting rid of his own pants, Mattie rolled down and reached for her purse. The bright blue wrapper was safely tucked away in the inner pocket, just as it always had been. A gasp escaped her lips when she came back up to find him just as naked as she was. "What?"

"Nothing," she assured him, suddenly mindful of the fact that she was staring intently between his legs.

"Here, give me that," he told her, reaching for the condom.

"No." She snatched it back out of his reach, and a smile spread across her lips. "Let me." Graham swallowed hard, trying to keep himself under reign as she rolled the thin latex over him. Her hands then ran up the length of his body to encircle his neck, which allowed her to pull him back on top of her.

The thought of *I can't believe this is happening* kept flashing through both their minds when he pushed his first thrust into her, and with each consequential one after that the thought faded. The heat of the moment brought both of them into complete single-mindedness, making them concentrate only on sound and touch and pleasure. She cried out when his grip on her got too tight, but the sensations of the ride soon drove it from her mind. And while it ended in a satisfying burst for him, it left her wanting.

When all was quiet again he started the soft, protective caressing that he now felt free to give. "Thank you," he whispered in her ear just before he kissed her neck. A gentle hand reached over to stroke her cheek as he continued to kiss her.

Mattie found her gaze boring into the ceiling. She noticed that she was suddenly cold, and her feelings about the man lying beside her were vastly different than they had been just an hour before. Her curiosity had finally been satisfied on the one question that had haunted her through most of their relationship. Now she had gotten her answer. "I have to go."

"What?" He pulled himself up onto an elbow so that he could look at her. "Already?" She nodded, then climbed out of bed to quickly dress. He sat up to follow her, but couldn't reach out to her. "Mattie, where are you going?"

"Vancouver," she grunted as she buttoned her blouse.

It only took a few seconds for her to finish, and she was swinging her purse up onto her shoulder when he finally reached for her elbow. "Wait a minute," he stopped her. "Didn't this mean anything to you?"

Mattie stared at him for a moment; deep down she wanted to be cruel, to hurt him just as much as he had hurt her for so many years. But she also felt a certain degree of compassion, and instead she sat down on the edge of the bed. "It did," she whispered, reaching up to run her fingers along his jaw. "I've always needed to know." A gentle kiss was her signal that the subject was not up for discussion, and this time when she stood, he didn't try to stop her. She turned at the door, and what she saw would be the image of him that would remain with her for the rest of her life; Graham sitting there naked – vulnerable – as he watched her go.

Chapter 33

Mattie squinted in the bright sunshine that bathed the coastline for the first time in nearly two weeks. Back in Alberta it was unusual to have two overcast days in a row. The rainy weather, unlike most, actually sent her spirits higher with excitement as she continued to explore her new home.

A concrete path wound along the edge of the beach, passing through both barren spots and small patches of wooded areas. As she strolled along, she inhaled deeply to enjoy the sea air. It was therapeutic for Mattie, and it brought a smile to her face every time she did it; it always reminded her that her life was now her own, and that she alone had made the decision to move here and start her life over again. And that it was the best decision she ever could have made. She had taken a job as an administrative assistant to pay the bills, then had thrown herself wholeheartedly into the local music scene. It paid off when she managed to secure a few engagements in small clubs and private functions, and she was even starting to build a small fan base.

She was set on autopilot, dreamily wandering along until she found a bench that overlooked the bay. Her purse fit neatly in the small space between where she sat and the iron railing that formed the arm rest. The wood was warm against her skin, inviting her to settle back, stretch her legs out and close her eyes.

The serenity was broken in an instant when she felt something collide heavily with her ankles. Her eyes flew open to find a man at her feet, on his hands and knees where he had landed after tripping over her sandals. "Oh my god!"

she gasped, clambering down to try and help him. "Are you okay?"

The man managed to sit back on his heels, but no further as he was hopelessly tangled in his dog's leash. He looked up to see what had caused him to fall, and found himself staring into her concerned eyes. He tried to answer, but his dog was pulling against his leash so hard that it pulled him off balance and he landed on his rear with a thud. "Jack!" he snapped at the retriever, who immediately stopped pulling and stared at him expectantly.

Mattie glanced at the dog, then back to the man. He was tall and lanky, almost gangly with limbs that looked like they shouldn't be able to coordinate into movement. His sandy hair had a bit of length, unruly in the breeze that had suddenly blown in off the water. The muscles that she could see peeking out from under his shirt rippled as he brushed the dust and pebbles from his hands. A couple of small red smudges streaked out across his palm, blood rising to the surface. "I'm so sorry," she apologized, crouching down to take a look at it.

Her touch shocked him, mostly because he was unaccustomed to complete strangers touching him. But when he looked up at her, he could see that she genuinely felt bad for tripping him. Her chin-length hair had fallen down into her mouth as she examined his hand, which she quickly tucked back behind her ear half a second before the wind blew it back in the way again. The hands that held his arm were strong, and she had instantly caught his attention. "It – it's my own fault," he stammered as he awkwardly tried to free himself from the leash. "I was watching him instead of looking where I was going."

They spent the next few moments taking in every detail of each other that they could get, and the silence was broken when the dog started to whine – distressed because the shortened leash prevented him from greeting the new stranger. "Jack…" he warned, giving the leash a short tug.

"It's okay." Despite her inherent fear of big dogs, she found herself smiling. The dog had taken the cue from his owner and sat down, so she felt relatively safe in extending her hand. Jack sniffed tentatively at it, taking his time in deciding that the stranger was indeed safe. Mattie laughed when he started licking her fingers. But her presence of mind returned, and she looked back at his hand. "I think you need a little first aid."

"No, I'm really okay," he told her.

She got back up to retrieve her purse from the bench, then sat down on the ground beside him as she dug into it. "I think I have some bandages in here somewhere."

"You don't have to do that," he told her as he used his good hand to continue untangling the leash.

"It's okay. It's the least I can do after trying to kill you."

Finally free, Jack scampered away to run off some energy. "Jack!" Mark hollered after him. "Come back here!" He started to laugh as he watched Jack sniff the trees, relieve himself, and then come thundering back after greeting a couple of other dogs along the way. He screeched to a halt, but sat down beside Mattie rather than in his usual place beside Mark.

Watching the dog had distracted Mattie from her search, but after petting Jack she finally found what she was looking for. "Ah hah! I knew I had put some of these in here." She took a couple of bandages out of the handful and handed them to him. "There you go."

"Thanks." He opened up the first package, giving her the scraps when she held out her hand and waited. The application was awkward – it was his dominant hand that had been hurt. She murmured an offer of help, then moved in to cover the wounds, unconsciously caressing his fingers briefly before catching herself and pulling back. With his good hand he reached across and told her, "My name's Mark."

She had to quickly shift everything around so that she could match him. "Mattie."

"I'd love to have the opportunity to pay you back for your kindness," he said, smiling as he brandished his bandaged hand.

"What kindness?" she countered. "I made you bleed." His only response was a shrug. Her smile faded momentarily, though she couldn't explain why. After a moment's consideration she agreed, "Okay. But you pick the place."

"How about Settaris? Eight o'clock Friday?"

"That sounds great." The grin returned fully. "I'll be the one with the big feet."

"Good. I'll see you then." He climbed to his feet and helped her up, then called for Jack. But Jack was reluctant to leave, staring intently at Mattie despite Mark's pulling on his leash.

She snickered, reaching down to hold the dog's face in her hands as she told him, "It's okay, pal. You can go." Her permission was all he needed, and they both laughed again when Jack obediently jumped up and followed Mark down the path. She settled back into the bench as she watched them go, then gazed back out over the water when she couldn't see them anymore.

He's an awfully nice man, El – a gentleman. We talked and talked for hours over dinner long after it had gone cold, leaving only because the restaurant closed. Then we moved to an all-night coffee shop, so it was nearly seven in the morning by the time I got home.

I really like him. I'd really like to date him. But Mark is still pretty broken up about his last

*girlfriend, who died from cancer a few years ago.
I don't think he's interested in dating anyone,
but I also think there's more to it than that. Even
if there wasn't anything, I'm not sure he would
want to date me.*

*But at least I've found a good friend, if
nothing else.*

Mattie flipped the page. The first picture Mark looked at was on the top left corner of the right page, a picture of his friend and a woman that he had never seen before. Mattie was dressed in a green, off-the-shoulder evening gown and the other woman was in a cream colored dress, the veil in her hair telling what the event was. "Who's that?" he asked.

"Who?" She scanned all the pictures, not sure of which one he was talking about.

"Her." He tapped the correct photo.

"Oh." There was a short pause before she answered. "That's Helen."

"Who's Helen?"

"A friend." She flipped to the next page, then to the next when she saw more pictures of her and Helen from varying points throughout their friendship. There was a bitter tone to her voice when she quietly added, "At least she used to be."

Mark watched her for a second or two. "You want to tell me about it?"

She handed the photo album to him in order to get up and grab her glass from the coffee table. "You want some more wine?" He nodded, and she headed around the corner and into the kitchen. Her voice was muffled by the drywall between them when she started to tell him the story. She didn't get into very much detail, but it got the point across anyway. She was back in the room when she finished with, "I haven't talked to her since."

"Oh." When she handed the album to him she had closed it, so Mark started at the beginning. He flipped on a couple of pages, and his eyes grew wide when he saw a newspaper article pasted in on the left side. "Oh my God..."

"What?" she asked, holding out his glass as she sat down beside him. He didn't answer, and she followed his stare to try and figure out the mystery as she set his wine down on the table. "See someone you know?"

A shaking finger pointed to the figure beside Mattie's ex-fiancé. "That – that's my sister."

"I think you're seeing things," she told him. "That's my ex's mistress."

For a split second Mark thought that he might possibly be mistaken. "What's her name?"

It had been so long since Mattie even thought about that time in her life that she hardly remembered anymore. "Maria...?" she tentatively offered. "Hawthorne...I think." She saw his expression turn to one of horror. "Your sister?"

Mark nodded slowly. "His name is John, right?"

"Yeah." She gaped at him, then at the picture, then back to him again. "I don't believe it." She put her own glass down before she could drop it. "It's impossible."

He took a deep breath. "He was at Maria's funeral, but I didn't know who he was." He paused, deciding whether he really wanted to get onto this topic, but eventually said, "She died..."

"In her car," she finished. "They thought that she deliberately asphyxiated herself."

The full weight of realization hit him, shaking hands dropping the album. "Oh God," he gasped, staring at her.

Tears started to well in her eyes. "I'm so sorry, Mark. I – I didn't know..."

"I've gotta go," he said suddenly, jumping to his feet and stepping on the album in his haste for the door. "I can't…"

"Wait a minute!" She quickly followed, but stopped short when she saw him scrambling into his jacket. "Mark, wait!"

"I gotta go," he repeated, nervous hands scratching for the doorknob. When it finally opened he whispered a hasty, "Bye," and bolted.

"Mark!" she called after him, futilely chasing him down to the front door. But he was too fast, and was long gone by the time she got there. "Mark!" She looked up and down the street for a few minutes, then sighed his name as she finally closed the door.

> Well El, my luck has struck again.
> I was going to ask him out this afternoon, but there's no way now. He freaked out – and I can't blame him. I'm a direct link to his dead sister.
> I'd be surprised if I ever saw him again. He…

A knock at the door lifted her pen in mid-stroke. She set the pen and book down, wondering who could possibly want to see her so late at night. She gasped, astonished when she saw him standing on the other side of the door.

He looked haggard, water still dripping down his face from the pouring rain outside. "Can I come in?" he asked quietly.

She nodded, extending her hand and pulling him inside. He stood in the entry as she closed the door, without direction until she guided him back to the leather couch. Mattie then made some tea, half-expecting him to be gone when she returned with his mug. But he was still there, lost in his own thoughts, letting her put the mug into his hands. She then sat down beside him – and waited.

It took a while, but he finally told her, "I haven't talked to anyone about her since she died." The mug turned in his hands. "I miss her so much."

She whispered, "You were close?"

"Uh huh." It took time, but he finally started to talk about her, telling Mattie about the close relationship they once had. He concluded when he told her, "I was so lucky to have her for my best friend. Until..."

"She met John." Mattie, for once, didn't feel the revulsion that usually accompanied his name. Her sadness for her friend far outweighed it.

He nodded. "It was like someone just flipped a switch. She was my sister one minute – then a stranger the next." He paused. "I don't know why she changed."

"She didn't mean to," Mattie suggested. "John had that effect on people. He was a good manipulator."

Mark finally looked at her, hoping for an explanation. "Yeah?"

With a small nod she told him, "I knew who I was before I met him. But by the end he had me second-guessing myself. He tried to make me have a baby I wasn't ready for, and then made me scared to tell anybody about it." She saw his jaw set hard, and she sympathized deeply. "You can't blame Maria. Whatever happened – she didn't deserve for it to end the way it did."

She watched him as he listened, never seeing such a lonely soul in her life. When she reached over to hug him he folded, grabbing desperately at the arm that reached around his front. "It's okay," she soothed, stroking his hair as he cried against her shoulder. "It's okay."

Chapter 34

Helen woke up around five in the morning, jolted from her sleep by the image of her son being hit by a truck. In a panic she rushed down the hall and into his room, to find the seven-year-old snuggled tightly against a tan-colored teddy bear that was larger than he was. His four-year-old sister Katrina remained undisturbed on the other side of the room, her thumb stuffed securely in her mouth. She breathed a sigh of relief and gently closed the door again, shaking her head at her own alarm. But the sudden rush of adrenaline made sleep out of the question.

She headed back to the bedroom to retrieve her robe, and in the dim moonlight that filtered through the window, she noticed that Kevin's side of the bed was undisturbed. Tying the fabric belt around her ever-expanding waist, she headed for the front entrance. His jacket and shoes were still gone, and the mat in the doorway was bone dry, devoid of any melted snow. A glance at the clock in the kitchen confirmed her worst fear – he hadn't come home that night.

Fury began to rise in her, making her hands shake and her heart pound in her ears. She paced repeatedly in a circle that took her from the front entrance into the kitchen, through the living room and back into the hallway. With every lap she got angrier and more disappointed – not just with her husband, but with herself. Somehow she had managed to allow things to slip to this point.

On one pass through the living room, her attention was caught by one of the pictures on the entertainment center. Her wedding day seemed to be hundreds of years before, not just the mere eight that the government knew about. In the center of the group were Helen and Kevin, flanked on one side by her brother and sister and on the other side by Kevin's best man and Mattie. Their hair was being tossed around by the wind, and with half a moment's smile Helen remembered how much trouble they had keeping her veil on her head that day.

The sentimentality disappeared in an instant. Her family lived nowhere near her, Mattie had dismissed her from her life, and her husband had betrayed her. Or more to the point, she finally allowed herself to acknowledge the fact that he'd been doing it for years. She actually preferred it when he didn't come home now, because then at least she wasn't at the mercy of his increasingly short temper.

A plan for leaving started to form in her head, but she abruptly shook it away when she realized that she had nowhere to go. Her brother and his wife lived in Toronto, her parents were in Nebraska, and what was left of her family was four hours away in Edmonton. Most importantly – she had no way of getting anywhere. No driver's license, no car and no money for her and the kids to take a bus. And in a town this small, there was no way for her to get any help.

The baby inside kicked the bottom of her rib. "It's alright," she soothed, rubbing her hand back and forth across her belly. "It's alright." Helen decided that she really needed to calm down, so she settled down on the couch with the afghan that was kept there. It took a minute or so for her to find a comfortable position, but when she was done she was able to stretch out and rest her head on the padded arm.

For a little while she tried to sleep, finally letting her eyes pop open when it wouldn't come. They started to dart around the room, and her ears perked up at the sound of a passing car. She knew that the car wasn't theirs, but as it went by it threw some light into the living room. She forgot everything else as a gold flash from the coffee table caught her attention. The light had bounced off his wedding ring, which sat in the center of the table's glass surface.

With a grunt of effort, Helen rolled forward to snatch the ring up. She turned it over and over in her hands, desperately trying to come up with reasons as to why he would leave his wedding ring behind. Any answer, other than the conclusion that she had already reached, would do. But as she continued to examine the fine detailing in the gold, her eyes started to well with tears. There was no other solution. Seemingly resigned to her fate, she placed the ring back on the table and returned to bed, only to cry herself to sleep.

Chapter 35

Mattie was singing her way through her weekly two-hour bubble bath when the phone in the kitchen started to ring. It rang three times before her voicemail picked it up, and once it stopped ringing she drew a deep breath and pulled her head beneath the suds. When forced to resurface, the dissolving bubbles that had been caught in her ears muted the sound of the still-ringing telephone. The voicemail picked up again, and a few minutes passed before the phone started ringing for the third time. "Oh for Christ's sake!" she groaned as she pulled herself from the water.

The ringing stopped as soon as she made it to the cell phone on her kitchen counter, nearly slipping on the linoleum with her wet feet. Muttering under her breath, Mattie readjusted the thick red cotton around her chest and waited. Just as she predicted, it rang again, but this time it took twice as long for the sound to start. The call display confirmed her suspicions. "What do you want, Mark?"

"How did you know it was me?" he asked, already sure of the answer.

Her eyes rolled. "If I could reach you, I'd soak you."

He laughed out loud. "Too bad I didn't come over to see you instead."

She found herself laughing despite her annoyance. "What do you want?"

"I just found out that I have to go to New York for a week for some business seminars," he said. "The company is paying for me and a companion. Wanna go?"

"New York?" she echoed excitedly. "When?"

"Three weeks from yesterday."

"Hang on a second." Mattie grabbed her daytimer from its place on the table and flipped a couple pages forward. "I think I can do it," she confirmed. "I'll just have to get the time off work."

"Perfect. This is going to be great."

She smiled. "Can I call you later? I'm about to flood out my kitchen."

"I'm going to be running around this afternoon. I'll call you tonight."

Mattie closed the phone and stood there a moment, her head filling with a million ideas. She returned to the tub, silently starting to organize everything she'd have to do before they left. The main thing that stood out was that she'd have to buy new pajamas – she hadn't bothered to replenish her lingerie wardrobe since she stopped seeing Zack. But the idea of shopping threw another wave of insecurities at her. She feared that Mark would get the wrong impression if she chose the wrong item. But she didn't want to share a room with him in hole-filled shorts and t-shirts either.

She groaned as her head rested against the tiles, musing, *Do pretty girls have this problem?* Then she chuckled to herself. *Of course they don't – they're sleeping with the men they travel with.*

Then she gave herself a mental kick. *There's nothing wrong with you!* She stared down at her body through the thin layer of bubbles, suddenly wondering just what it was she was trying to hide.

And what exactly it was that she wanted to hide from Mark.

It had been hard at first, but with practice, Mattie had learned not to fantasize about him. Initially she felt herself falling into the same traps that she had with Graham and John – even Zack, to some extent. It was an effort not to read too much into anything he said, especially since he was a natural flirt. She had to constantly remind herself that the innuendo between them was just that. She was comfortable with him, he was safe – and she wasn't about to let anything change that. Their friendship was too much to risk.

But it wasn't going to keep her from an all-expense paid trip to the Big Apple either.

Mark was intent on making the flight to New York an eventful, if not entertaining one. They started by having a couple of drinks at the airport before boarding, and then they carried on a lighthearted banter from the moment they took off until they arrived at the hotel. It kept him focused, and from falling apart from nerves.

About a month before, the two of them had been spending a Saturday morning together at the farmer's market. It hadn't been an unusual day, but as they walked between the stalls he found himself gazing at her, and something occurred to him that hadn't before. He felt completely at ease with her, an ease that he had never felt with anyone – not even with Sasha. But there was something more about Mattie, and it threw him into deep contemplation. The whole reason for inviting her on this trip was to spend some genuine one-on-one time with her, to see if what he was feeling was merely infatuation or something more. And if it was infatuation, then he would let it go and never allow himself to say anything to her.

They arrived at the hotel at midnight and checked in with little difficulty, riding up to their floor in silence. Mattie didn't even attempt to stifle her yawn as they walked through the hallways, trying to find the right door. He couldn't help but smirk when he asked, "Tired?"

She gave him a wan smile, then checked the room number again as they turned another corner. "There it is." When they got inside, they found a short hallway that led into a large sleeping area. The room was tastefully decorated, though a little out of date, comfortably cool from the air conditioner, and not the double that they had asked for. "Uh oh."

Mark was a few steps behind, making sure all their bags were inside before closing the door. "What's wrong?" When she didn't answer, he came up behind her to see what was bothering her.

There weren't the two double beds that had been on their original reservation, just one king. Both vaguely wondered if the other had called ahead and changed the room request, but dismissed the idea – it wasn't something either of them would do. "So now what?" she wondered aloud, just staring at the bed.

"I guess we share," he told her, also staring in the same direction. "Unless you want me to sleep on the floor."

"No, that's okay." She turned to pick up her suitcase, but found that he was still gazing absently at the bed. Mattie could tell that he was lost, and a thought entered her mind. *He hasn't shared a bed with anyone since Sasha.* Mattie carefully reached a hand up to rest it on his chest. "Mark?"

Her touch was enough to pull him back into the room, and with a sudden pang of panic, he found himself wondering what exactly he was doing. *This is crazy,* he told himself with a slight shake of his head. Then he realized that she was watching him, a worried expression on her face. "Sorry," he apologized, a tinge of color flushing his cheeks.

She frowned. "You okay?"

"I'm fine," he said, pulling a lung full of air into his chest. She was still unsure, so he briefly touched her shoulder to assure her that he was telling the truth. Then after breaking into an unconvincing smile he asked, "Which side do you want?"

The pair filled the next hour or so with idle conversation, an unintentional ploy to avoid the fact that they needed to share the bed. But both had to eventually concede exhaustion. Mattie excused herself and went into the washroom to change, looking skeptically at her new blue nightgown as she held it out in front of her. She had spent a good hour in the store agonizing over a few choices, finally settling on this one after getting an opinion from every clerk there. She started to put it on, but then thought differently of it when she remembered Mark's change of mood just a few minutes before. The blue nightgown was carefully folded and put away, and instead she changed into a tank top and pair of shorts.

They finally climbed under the covers after what had become a very long, although pleasant, day together. Some tossing and turning accidentally knocked them together, nervous laughter erupting from both of them. With the tension broken, Mattie rolled onto her side and faced away from him.

Mark snuggled in close behind her and laid his arm over her side, her head resting just beneath his chin. He could feel her fingertips absently drifting back and forth across his forearm, and she could feel his grip around her waist tighten just a little. Mattie sighed and willed herself to sleep, but her eyes had different ideas and instead started to wander around the darkened room.

Behind her, Mark was doing the same thing, but was lost in his own thoughts again. He was rethinking the whole idea, though he wasn't sure why. There was no reason for him to doubt that she liked him – laying back into his arms was proof of that. But it did little to dispel his anxiety. He tried to open his mouth half a dozen times, wanting to just blurt out his intentions. But the words wouldn't come.

It took a couple of hours, but Mark could hear her breathing even out as sleep started to claim her. She shifted a little, rolling back against him as she murmured, "I'm glad you asked me to come with you."

Her soft voice shocked him, as he had been starting to fall asleep himself. "So am I," he whispered, laying a gentle kiss on the top of her head. *I just hope I'm right.*

Chapter 36

Saturday was a bright, sunny day as Mark and Mattie walked west from their hotel to Central Park. Their conversation was light, and though he was able to make himself appear carefree, inside he was tied up in knots. Today was the day – he knew that he had to say something. He was just looking for the right moment now.

The couple stopped at a hot dog cart, then slowly made their way to a bench that overlooked a reed-encircled pond. A habitual quick eater, Mark finished way ahead of his friend, and he used the time it took to walk to the nearest trash can to gather his thoughts. When he came back, she had stretched her legs out over the length of the bench. He stood there, staring at her. She grinned and told him, "I didn't want to trip you."

Mark gave a nervous laugh, waiting for her to pull her feet away so he could sit down, and then letting her rest her heels on his thighs once he was settled again. They sat in silence for a long time – hers comfortable and his filled with tension – just soaking up the first sunshine they had seen all week. Despite the fact that he was there to attend seminars, he actually only made it to one. The rest of the week had been devoted to spending time with Mattie, just to be sure that it was indeed love that he was feeling for her. Even he was amazed that he had kept it together for so long without letting his feelings slip. There had been one occurrence when she asked him if something was on his mind, but he denied it, and she never brought the subject up again.

They were leaving in two days, and he was really hoping to treat her to one night of romance in the Big Apple.

His hands held a loose grip on her feet, and after a while his thumb started absently rubbing back and forth over her skin. *It's now or never.* After a deep breath he slowly questioned, "What would you say if...I told you I had another reason for asking you to come to New York?"

The movement of her jaw stopped, leaving a large lump of food for her to swallow before she could answer him. Mark was barely able to hear her when she asked, "Like what?"

He had managed to build a little courage, enough that he could look directly into her eyes when he told her, "I...I think..." He stopped, cleared his throat, then said, "I'm in love with you, Matt. I have been since the day I met you." He watched in agony as she gaped at him without a word. After a long silence he finally asked, "Aren't you going to say anything?"

It was clear that he had stunned her, not because the news had come out of the blue, but because his behavior all week should have tipped her off. She felt stupid – that she'd somehow led him on after consciously deciding that she wouldn't let them jeopardize their friendship. And she got angry at herself for allowing it to happen. "How?" she gasped. "How can you?"

It hung in the air between them for a long time. "I don't know," he eventually said. "But I do."

"But I – Maria –" Mattie suddenly had a flashback, to the night on her balcony when Graham told her that he didn't love her. "Oh no."

Mark's heart leapt up into his throat. He had thought about this so much, and in every fantasy her eyes had lit up and she had jumped into his arms in agreement. A shake of his head helped to confirm what she had really said. "Oh no?" he murmured. "What do you mean oh no?"

His admittance of love had thrown her into a daze, and she could feel the tug of a whirlpool at her feet. She had thought about it, and she wanted it. But history was always doomed to repeat itself, and the cold, hard instinct that she had steadfastly built around herself since her last great romance had immediately fallen into place as soon as she had realized that she had started falling for him months before. She started to say something, closed her mouth again, then opened up to say, "I..."

His face dropped, traumatized. Defeat came to him quickly, and with his head hung and eyes staring at the walking path he whispered, "You don't feel the same."

"It's not that," she said, pulling her feet from his grasp and putting them on the ground.

"Then what?"

"Well..." The word had come out of her mouth before she had thought of the follow-up for it. To stall for time, she stood up and started to pace across a small section of asphalt in front of the bench. "It's so hard to describe," she tried to get him to understand. "It's...it's..." Try as she might, the words just would not come out in a properly arranged order, opting to stick inside her chest.

Mattie was grasping at straws, which was painfully obvious to Mark. He couldn't understand it. She was warm, she was loving; she had never given any indication that she didn't want the exact same thing that he wanted. *Then again,* he thought to himself, *she's never really given me a reason to think so either.* Frustration started to build inside him, and he also started reaching for reasons. "Is it someone else?"

She stopped cold, hurt plain in her face. "There is no one else – you know that."

At wit's end, he challenged, "If you don't love me, then just say so."

Her eyes flashed. "I do love you!"

The vehemence of her answer caught them both off guard. He got his answer, but not in the way it was supposed to come. "Then what's the problem?"

She really didn't have a good answer. "I don't deserve you."

"That's not true and you know it."

She stomped a foot, clearly frustrated at not being able to control her feelings or come up with the right words. Her pacing started again. Her secret fantasy had the potential to become reality, and all she could think about was what had happened in the past. She had been told she'd been loved so many times, and it never led to anything but heartbreak. Finally she said, "Do you know how many times someone's told me this?"

"What are you saying?" he countered. "You don't believe me?" She wasn't able to answer him, words caught in her throat. He walked over to her, his voice low when he told her, "I'm not going to do what they did." Not knowing what else to do, she turned her back on him to keep him from seeing the tears forming in her eyes. Before he could even think of what he really was meaning to say he demanded, "Why am I paying for other men's mistakes with you?" She didn't say anything, but the confused shake of her head drove his anger up another notch. "First John promises to marry you while he's still sleeping with my sister," he lectured, "and then you let Graham string you along for seven years without ever telling you if he loved you or not."

"But what if you don't?" she finally countered. Her thoughts flew back to that final night on her balcony with Graham, and how it had destroyed her happiness for years afterward. "What if you just think you do now, but you find out in a couple of years that it wasn't such a good idea? I can't go through that again, Mark. I just can't."

He started to get angry at her doubt of his sincerity. "Why don't you believe me?"

"Because I believed everyone else!" she snapped, whirling back at him. "I gave it my all and I was always the one who ended up getting killed."

"So you're going to walk away from me because of what those guys did to you?" He had had enough. "Do you think you're the only one that's ever been hurt?" he snapped, closing the distance between them again. "At least you haven't watched someone you love die. At least you didn't kill them!" His voice stopped as he realized what he had just said, suddenly discovering that he was not healed nearly as well as he liked to think. He turned his back on her, a soft curse going with him.

She was not making any sense in her head, so Mattie knew that she was definitely not making any sense in this argument. She wasn't even sure why it had turned into an argument. Her friend had declared his love for her. His love... "No, I haven't," she admitted quietly. Now uncomfortable being as close to him as she was, Mattie started down the path toward the ivy-covered stone bridge.

Not willing to accept defeat, he chased after her. "Matt, I don't know any other way to tell you that I love you. What do you want me to do? Mattie, stop!" He cut her off, catching her by the arm to hold her in place. "Is there some test I have to take? Do I have to do a fire walk? Do I have to go beat the shit out of every guy who ever broke your heart?"

"Alright, enough!" She shot him a glare of contempt as she broke free from his grip, but she stayed within the same five feet this time. Her back turned to him as pieces of past romances flashed before her. Without warning, she sank to the grass and started to cry.

Mark was unsure of what to do now, but he thought that moving toward her would be a good start. He crouched down beside her and tentatively rested his hand on her shoulder. "Matt?"

At the sound of her name she immediately straightened up, hurriedly wiping her tears away. "I'm sorry."

He drew his hand back as soon as she moved, but didn't budge from his spot. "Don't be sorry," he whispered.

"I hate it when I do this."

"I know."

"No you don't." She was up on her feet in an instant, now pacing in a circle around him. Her chest was about to burst with anxiety, and the nerves were enough to tighten her throat. "Do you know how many times someone has told me that they loved me?"

"Why are we going back to this?"

She shot him a glare. "Just answer my question."

"How should I know?"

"But you do know," she reminded him. "I've told you about every one of them. And it isn't that many." A fresh flow of tears started to roll down her cheeks, but she turned herself around so that she could face him again. "They devastated me, Mark. I don't know if I can go through that again."

"Hey…." His expression softened, and as he reached up for her hands he realized just what she was trying to say. "What makes you think that it's going to happen again?"

She shrugged, but let him pull her down to sit in front of him as she whimpered, "It always does."

"Don't you think that this is hard for me too?" For once in his life, Mark knew exactly what to say next. "I was with Sasha for six years. And it took me that long to figure out that I wasn't in love with her. I never was – I only stayed with her because she was sick. But even with all that, I still didn't want anyone after she died." He rested his hands on her knee. "But when I met you, I started to feel again. And I finally realized that what I felt for you was love." Mark looked at her, ducking his head a little to catch her eye. "You can't tell me you haven't thought about it."

"I have," she admitted softly, slowly nodding her head. They had reached the moment that she had hoped would never appear in her life again – when she would have to decide whether it was worth it to overstep the bounds of friendship to follow her heart. Last time she had done it freely, without hesitation. Now, Mattie found that the decision had become critical. Mark meant so much more to her than Graham ever did. "Do you really love me?" she asked him, her expression brightening into a small smile.

Mark suddenly found that he had unconsciously been biting the side of his tongue. "I do," he confirmed, his own relieved smile now returning hers. "I'm sure of it."

She drew in a breath to steady herself, then leaned forward and gently kissed him, still somewhat surprised when he kissed her in return. They then held onto each other for a little while, alone together, surrounded by the sounds of the park.

Shaking hands set Mattie's brush down on the bathroom counter later that night. She looked in the mirror one last time to check her hair, then walked into the bedroom, stopping just inside the door. Mark was sitting in bed, his back against the headboard as he absently read through his notes from the one seminar he had managed to attend. He looked up when she came in, letting out a low whistle as he set the papers down on the mattress. She was dressed in a flowered robe with black trim and bare feet, her hair falling down gently around her face. The nerves were very obvious as her fingers toyed with the robe's belt. "You look beautiful," he breathed as he flipped the covers back and got up.

She forced a small smile. "Do I meet with your expectations?"

He could see the worry in her face, so to break the tension he flapped his arms, crossed his hands in front of his waist and adopted a rapper tone when he told her, "Yo, you're hot."

Mattie burst into laughter as he moved in on her, pushing away from him when he grabbed her. "You're crazy!"

"Werd." He kissed her before she could think of anything else to say, feeling her tension beginning to melt away as she tentatively pressed up against him. When they parted, he held her face in his hands and just looked into her eyes for a moment. He wasn't sure why, but he was feeling differently about her now – not in a bad way, but strange nonetheless.

Mattie found him staring at her with a look that she'd never seen from any man before. It didn't scare her, but it did add to the intensity of the situation. Unsure of her next move, she felt more nervous than ever. And when he reached down to untie her robe, she tensed right back up. "What's wrong?" he asked, quickly pulling away.

"I'm scared," she murmured.

"How come?"

"I…" She glanced around her, not really seeing anything as she concentrated on trying to get the words out. She wanted to go slowly, to relish the experience, to make sure that this ended so much better than all the others had. The sentences formed in her head over and over again, but the filter between her brain and mouth – which usually didn't work – seemed to have strengthened to full capacity. Try as she might, she couldn't articulate what she was feeling. So in an attempt to deflect the truth, she smiled and told him, "It's just that – it's been a while since I did this."

"Oh Matt." He gave her an understanding smile, then lifted her chin up so he could kiss her once again. As they embraced he lifted her off her feet and carried her over to the bed, where she landed on the stack of papers he had left behind. Extracting them created another humorous, yet awkward moment between them – he had managed to pin her and she wasn't able to remove the papers on her own. Finally she surrendered and asked for, "A little help?"

Mark lifted himself off of her, then removed the notes as she arched her back. The robe now fell open, revealing the navy blue nightgown she had hidden underneath. He

208 ~ KAYT ROTH

grinned, and for comic flair he tossed the papers over his head and across the room, then came back down to kiss her again. He could see that she was still concerned, so he assured her, "Don't worry – it's just like riding a bicycle."

Now she couldn't help but smirk. "I haven't been on one of those in a while either." He laughed, but his laughter faded when she touched his face and said, "I think we might both be a little wobbly in the beginning."

Mark faltered, flashing back to one of his last memories with Sasha – the day she told him of her dream about his future. He thought it odd that he should think of it now, but he realized why. Mattie meant moving on, whether he was ready to or not. He never realized until now how far he'd been in denial of Sasha's impact on him.

When his thoughts returned him to the present, he found Mattie's eyes nervously staring up at him. Finally he whispered, "Maybe wobbly, but still standing."

Her eyes welled with tears, which ran down her cheeks when she pulled him close. For a little while they lay together in silence, listening to the other breathe. Mattie stared at the ceiling, thinking back to their argument that afternoon. "I'm sorry for what I said today," she murmured after a while. "It's not how I pictured that moment happening."

"Me either." Her words had jolted him out of his own memories of that day. "I saw it having balloons and a parade."

She started laughing, then rolled onto her side so she could look him in the eye. "Is this why you asked me to come to New York with you?"

Even in the limited light she could see Mark blush a little, which confirmed what she had been thinking ever since their fight in the park. "Are you mad?" he asked.

She shook her head. "I'm glad you did. I never would have said anything."

He came up and kissed her gently, sighing when she started to run her fingers up into his hair. Then he rolled onto his back and took her hand to invite her up on top. Mattie seated herself across his hips, taking the opportunity to toss her robe off the end of the bed. Then she came down and kissed him hard, full of the passion that she had always known resided within her somewhere. The terror of stepping beyond their friendship still sat in the back of her mind, but its intensity was fading quickly. It wasn't so much Mark's convincing that was doing it, but something inside of her just decided that it was time to let go of the fear and the apprehension that had kept her from being happy for the last few years.

He worked his way down her neck, gently pulling her from her thoughts when his lips started to push against the top of her nightgown. Mattie sat up and brought him with her, and she could feel his hands start slide underneath the hem at her knees. She reached down to remove the satin slip, but his hands were quick. "Don't…" he breathed. For a moment she stared at him, confused. He saw this and smiled. "Later."

She broke into a slow, tender smile and nodded. Her fingers remained in his grip, and he locked them together with his as the others reached up to run through her hair. Her eyes slid closed as her free hand slid up his arm, just reveling in the sensation. Mark kissed her again softly, remaining there for the longest time as he just kissed her. They had all the time in the world, and he was not about to let her rush through something as important to both of them as this.

The fact that they had slowed down considerably was not lost on Mattie, and she unwillingly flashed back to the night she spent with Graham. What they had done then was fast and hard, with nothing but pent-up, residual tension fuelling them. It was no wonder she had felt nothing toward him afterward. Without realizing it, she pulled away to gaze at the man who was with her now. He had been more than understanding with her, but it had taken the argument that afternoon to set everything in motion. *Funny how something like this comes out of hostility,* she thought to herself.

"Matt?" he whispered, looking deep into eyes that were focused on nothing.

She drew an involuntary breath, now actually seeing him in the moment rather than earlier that afternoon. "Sorry," she said sheepishly, her gaze flicking down to the nonexistent space between them. "I was just thinking."

"About what?"

Hesitation filled her, making her wonder if telling him what she had been reflecting on was a smart idea. There wasn't much choice though – starting this relationship was beginning to act like truth serum. "About…"

The silence of the small hotel room enveloped them, and when she didn't continue, he helped dissipate her tension with another kiss. "It's okay," he assured her. "You'll tell me when you're ready."

Her response was to kiss him, and to set everything into motion again. She desperately wanted to shed the nightgown, to hold his chest tight to her own. But he had asked, and he was the one setting the pace now. So she waited, letting him tease her into near ecstasy without removing anything. When the fabric was finally pulled off her body, she shuddered with delight.

His mouth found hers, and with firm hands on her back he tried to take her with him as he rolled down onto the mattress. She braced her arms, locking them at the elbows and suspending herself above him as his head hit the pillow. At least that's what she attempted to do. But it wasn't the graceful movement that it was intended to be, and she fell heavily against him when a slippery sheet pulled one arm out from under her. Mark suddenly found himself out of breath with a mouthful of her long hair, and she broke into deep, genuine laughter when he started to spit it out.

Mark dropped his head back with a groan as laughter consumed her, and soon he was laughing just as hard as she was. She rested her head on his chest, remaining there for a while when they both seemed to lapse into a quiet lull. "I'm sorry," she eventually murmured, her voice muffled by him.

"For what?"

She lifted her head to look at him, searching his eyes to see if he really didn't understand. She wasn't even sure herself, or more to the point, wasn't sure how to explain it. Sex was supposed to be serious – at least it had always been in her experience. John had been proof of that. Even Zack had lapsed into a reverent sort of lovemaking once he really got involved. Mattie's brow furrowed, and she tried to think of the best way to say it. The best she could come up with was, "For ruining the mood."

Now he understood, and it caused him to chuckle. "It's going to take a lot more than that to throw me off." After affording himself a moment just to look at her, in a flash he pulled her across him and rolled her over onto the other side of the bed. Then he started a merciless session of tickling and teasing, the kind that kept her laughing as he began to show her exactly what she had been missing.

Helen paced her traditional path through the townhouse, barely avoiding the toys that the kids had missed picking up before they went to bed. Nerves caused her to chew ruthlessly at her nails, her heart pounding in her ears. She jumped when the timer went off, but paused for a moment before she went back through the bathroom door.

The test sat on the counter where she had left it, now displaying the two lines that would change her life for the fourth time. Her hand flew to her mouth when she saw it, and all she could murmur was, "Oh god, not again."

Mark awoke with a start at the sound of his cell phone ringing. He squinted at the bright light that was pouring through the gaps in the curtains, nearly blinded as his hand reached around the nightstand to find it. He tried looking at the call display through sleepy eyes, but couldn't make out the words. "What?"

"Mark?"

"Yeah," he affirmed, quickly growing tired of waiting to see who it was. "What do you want?"

"Mark, it's Mom."

His heart froze – the call a chilling reminder of the day that his sister died. "Mom? What time is it?"

"It's eight-thirty." He could almost hear her smiling through the phone. "Are you still asleep?"

Which meant that it was eleven-thirty in New York. "I was." Now the brightness of the room made sense. But the memory of that day many years before had scared him. "Is everything okay?"

"Oh, everything's fine." Doris Layton sat back in her chair, using the handle of her coffee cup to pull it across the table toward her. "I just wanted to call and see how you were doing."

His head hit the wooden headboard with a gentle thud. "And to see if I was in the middle of something," he suggested.

On the other end of the line, his mother smirked as she agreed, "Something like that."

Mattie was still asleep beside him, her arm tucked up under her pillow and facing away from him. "We're in the middle of wild, abandoned sex with some friends of ours," he told her.

His attempt to get a rise of embarrassment out of her failed miserably. "Well that's good to know," she said flatly, a smile still playing at her lips. "Give me a call when you're finished."

"Okay, I will," he told her with a nod. "I'll talk to you later." Mark leaned over to put the phone back on the nightstand, sitting in thought for a few minutes before taking a look at his companion. She was peaceful, lost in the same kind of slumber that he had just been rousted from. He settled back down, but when sleep didn't overtake him, he rolled over and just gazed at her.

"Stop watching me," she murmured, barely loud enough for him to hear.

He blushed a little at being caught. But he kissed the back of her shoulder instead, whispering, "I can't sleep."

She rolled over to meet Mark's eyes, his head propped up on his arm as he looked at her. "Morning," she whispered, a sleepy smile instantly appearing on her face.

"It's almost noon." He reached down to stroke her hair and marveled, "God, you're beautiful."

"Even now?" He nodded, and raised up to kiss him. "I just wanted to make sure." Mark laughed and kissed her again, and when they parted she took on a serious tone when she asked, "Everything okay with your mom?"

He did a bit of a double take. "You heard that?" She just smiled, and his eyebrow lifted along with his own smile. "Everything's fine. She just wanted to catch me in the middle of something."

She sat up a little, grinning from ear to ear when she said, "I would have given her something to interrupt, but I was just too tired. Yesterday was a very eventful day." After one more kiss she threw back the covers. "Come on, I'm hungry."

Mattie didn't even get both feet off the mattress before he snatched her up by the waist and hauled her back down beside him, ruthlessly tickling along the way. "Let's stay," he suggested, pausing his torture only long enough for her to hear him before resuming his attack. "We'll call room service."

Mattie gasped for breath between bursts of hysterical laughter, only half-heartedly trying to push him away from her. "Hey! Knock it off!" He paused long enough to let her catch her breath, then attacked her neck with gentle teeth. "Mark, I'm starving," she protested, not really meaning it any more than she had two minutes before.

"Oh come on," he whined as he pulled her close. "Don't make me bring the white rapper out again."

It didn't take long for us to settle into a comfortable relationship, and I have to admit that I can't remember the last time I had so much fun. I wish I could put it into words so that you could understand just how I feel – but then again, if your feelings for Kevin are even remotely like it, then I guess I don't have to.

It propelled me into a creative blur, though I fully admit that most of what's coming out of my head these days is pure mush. But I figure what the hell – after all that the two of us have been through, we're entitled. He's actually pretty comfortable with elements of his life and our relationship finding their way into my work, more than I would have thought. Some people have been pretty touchy about that sort of thing in the past.

We bought a house together this past fall, a cozy little place that Mark had been keeping his eye on for the last few years. It's in a quiet residential area, with a park nearby for dog

*running. But his faithful companion Jack died
from old age about three months ago. I miss the
old lug terribly, and I've never seen Mark so
distraught. He was like a mother looking for her
kitten that's been given away. It took me a while,
but I finally figured out a way to hopefully raise
his spirits.*

Mattie glanced up at the clock when she heard a kick on the door. It was nine o'clock, and Mark was right on time. She gave herself one last glance in the hallway mirror, then checked through the peephole before opening the door.

He was on the front step just as she had expected, drenched from the day-long rain but in good spirits. In one hand a large, white plastic bag contained their Chinese food for dinner, and in the other he was barely managing to hold onto the three movies that he had rented. "Hi there," he greeted warmly when he saw her. Her newly colored hair jumped out at him, forcing him to examine her for any other changes she may have made. "You look great," he finally told her.

"Thanks," she grinned, absently tucking a piece of hair back behind her ear. She couldn't hide her amusement when she told him, "You look wet."

"Thanks. I did it specially for you." He stepped inside and handed the food to her so that she could take it into the kitchen. "I got some extra soy sauce," he told her as he dug through the closet for a hangar.

"We already have some," she called back from the kitchen. When she came back to the door, he was trying to untie his shoe without kneeling down, and was hopping to keep his balance. Mattie folded her arms across her chest and leaned up against the wall when she commented, "That's an interesting dance."

"Fertility," he said without looking up.

Her smug expression disappeared as soon as he said it. "What?"

"Fertility." The shoe finally came off, and he tossed it over into the corner with the first one. He stood up and deadpanned, "It helps ensure a good evening."

Now Mattie was able to put the smugness back onto her face. "Oh you think so, do you?"

He walked up to her and wrapped his hands around her waist to pull her close. "Absolutely." He kissed her, but barely got into it before she pushed him away with a giggle. "You don't believe me," he said.

"Not for a minute." When he leaned down to kiss her again, Mattie ducked out of his grasp. "Come on," she told him as she headed back into the kitchen. "I'm hungry."

He followed her into the kitchen and started unpacking the containers. Mattie reached for plates when she asked, "So did you confirm that toothpaste account?"

"They came in and signed all the paperwork today. And…" He traded her a plate for aluminum bowl of fried rice. "They want to use your jingle for it."

Mattie's face lit up. "Really?" She eagerly hugged him, nearly dropping the container in the process. "What about your boss? What did he say?"

He grinned again. "He says that a couple more deals like this would give me a partnership. And if that happens, I'll finally have enough holiday weeks to drive to the east coast."

She handed over the lemon chicken that he was pointing to. "The east coast?"

"Yeah, I've always wanted to drive across…" The words trailed off as his attention shifted. "Did you hear that?"

"Hear what?"

He listened again, eyes narrowing to slits in concentration. "I thought I heard a puppy."

"I didn't hear anything."

A loud whimper filled the air to contradict her, accompanied by scratching. Mark set his plate down on the counter, carefully so not as to interrupt what he was trying to hear. "There it is again." The whimpering grew louder, prompting him out of the kitchen.

"Where's it coming from?" she pondered, following him back into the foyer.

"Sounds like the front door." He opened the door and stuck his head out, but there was nothing there. New rivulets of rainwater streaked down his face when he came inside, but he didn't notice them. "Why do I still hear a puppy?"

"Maybe that's because there *is* a puppy."

He frowned at her, seeing only a pleasant smile on her face until she pointed to the laundry room. A chocolate lab pup came tumbling out when Mark opened the door, and once it regained its footing it immediately lumbered over to the man that had freed it. Mark crouched down and took the pup, then looked back up. "Matt – what did you do?"

She leaned against the doorframe, her arms folded across her chest as she gazed at them. "I know how much you miss Jack – I miss him too. And I know that this isn't him, but I thought he'd make a nice addition to the family."

Settaris, which was now an hour's drive away from Mark and Mattie's new home, was crowded the following Saturday night. It was rare for them to come back into her old neighborhood, but at his suggestion they took dinner near the same place that they had met three years before. Mark kept glancing nervously around the room all night, a behavior that was not missed by his girlfriend. She watched him for a little while, consciously trying to hide her amusement. They were about halfway through their desserts when she couldn't take the suspense any more. "Mark?" she called quietly, purposely keeping a light tone.

He looked up from his cake with a bit of surprise. "Huh?"

She set her spoon back down into the parfait glass. "Everything alright?"

"Fine," he answered, cursing inwardly when he realized how quick he had been to respond to her question. In an attempt to gain a smooth recovery, he adopted an air of indifference and said, "Why do you ask?"

The beginning of a smile started to pull at the corner of her mouth, her unflinching gaze making him fidget. "You seem a little nervous, that's all."

"Nervous?" He thought about it for a moment, the best lie he could come up with being, "I guess I'm just a little on edge. It was a pretty rough day."

The curl of her lip turned into a full-fledged smile. "I imagine it has been," she said, not at all lost on the double meaning her words implied. Mark's brow furrowed, her comment not lost on him either. He decided to ignore it for the time being and just concentrate on getting through dinner.

It only took a few more minutes for their waiter to come back, and he was able to settle their bill quickly after. He offered his arm to her once they were outside, smiling when she took it without hesitation. They walked through the parking lot, her curiosity piqued quite a bit more when they went right past the car and out into the dark walking paths that extended along the beach. The path disappeared into a large bank of trees, continuing on in nearly pitch black conditions for a good twenty minutes. Normally Mattie would become nervous in such an environment, but Mark put his arm tightly around her shoulders, which was more than enough to calm her anxiety.

The path left the forest when it reached a strategically placed lookout on the westernmost point. The Pacific Ocean beat softly against the rocks, while the twinkle of cities across the bay rose up against the mountains. It was a clear night with a full moon, bright enough to bathe them in shades of blue light, and it was silent except for the sound of the water on the shore.

Mattie tightened her grip around his waist just a little bit, bringing her other arm around his front to hug him. They hadn't been here in almost two years, and the view was just as beautiful as she remembered it. "We should come here more often," she suggested.

He nodded his agreement before gently pulling himself out of her grip. Without a word he led her over to the single wooden bench behind them – the one that she had originally tripped him from. He sat her down, then slowly dropped down beside her. "Matt," he started, taking her hands into his, "I wanted to bring you back to the place where we first met." He looked around to indicate the lookout point, her eyes following his. Mark looked back at her, but she was still gazing out over the calm sea.

A squeeze on her hands brought her eyes back to his, in time to catch him swallow hard and take a deep breath. For about the hundredth time, he caught himself doubting that he would ever be able to get the words out of his mouth. When he saw her sweet, patient smile, his confidence was boosted. "I've never felt this way for anyone before," he said, falling back into his carefully rehearsed speech, "and I was lucky enough to find a woman who feels the same way about me. I love you so much." He could see the tears already forming in her eyes as he slid off the edge of the bench and went down on one knee in front of her to ask, "Marry me?"

Mattie had known exactly what he was going to say, partially from intuition and mostly because of the way he had been acting all night. Nonetheless, she noticed her own jaw drop, and the sudden blurred image of his face when unshed tears got in the way. He was ready to explode, his eyes desperately searching her expression for an answer. A shaking hand left his grip to caress his cheek, which filled the time that it took for her to find her voice again. "Yes," she whispered. She got louder when she said again, "Oh Mark, yes."

My Dearest Helen,

It's 4 am on the morning of my wedding. I can't sleep. I'm not nervous – I am excited. It's already becoming the most wonderful day of my life. I can see why you looked forward to it the way you did. Mark is an incredible man – so patient and understanding.

After all, he'd have to be to deal with me, wouldn't he?

I wish more than anything that you could be here with me now. It's the one thing that will keep this day from being absolutely perfect. But even though I long ago resigned myself to what I did, I never doubt that we'll see each other again one day.

In the meantime, I will continue to miss you.

All my love,
Mattie

Chapter 37

Mark paid for his cab and pulled his suitcase through the front door, surprised to see that there were no lights on at eight-thirty at night. Mattie was nowhere to be found, but she had left behind a large assortment of papers and catalogues scattered across the living room. Odie had laid himself on top of them when he stretched out for a nap on the couch, a number of them falling to the floor when he got down to greet his master. Once Mark finished petting the dog, he took a minute to examine what Mattie had been looking over – information about attending a number of different universities. His brow furrowed, and he called out, "Matt?"

"Yeah?" her voice came from the other end of the house.

"I'm back!" He returned to the entrance to hang up his coat and, then came back in the living room to turn on some lights. She came out a short while later, and from her expression only he would know that she had been crying that afternoon; her eyes were still a little red to go along with the slight congestion that was left over. He took her into her arms and kissed her before he asked, "What's the matter?" Mattie didn't answer, but just shook her head a little. He led her back to the couch and sat her down beside him, and he asked her again, "What's the matter?"

She gestured over to the coffee table. "I just spent the afternoon looking through all of these," she told him sadly. "I've had an epiphany."

"You're giving up?" he questioned when realization set in. She nodded again, and he took her hands into his as he asked her, "Why?"

Her eyes instantly welled up with tears, a fresh flow that after her last three hours of crying she didn't think was possible. "I'm sick of fighting," she managed to get out of her tightened throat. "I'm sick of fighting for a job, and then fighting off everyone once I get it."

"But you're so good at it," he pointed out.

"No I'm not."

Mark frowned at her again. "You're one of the best performers I've ever seen." She shook her head, and he questioned, "How come you never said anything about this before?" The box of tissues that she had been using earlier in the afternoon was still sitting on the coffee table, so he grabbed one and handed it to her.

"I wasn't sure," she told him as she took one to dry her eyes. "But I've been thinking about it for a while." He remained silent, letting her tell him in her own good time. She took a little while to clean herself up before saying anything else. "Is it crazy," she mused, "to want something so badly that you continue to pursue it even though it seems like you have no hope of ever getting it?"

"Not really." He was searching his brain for something to say that would make her feel better. As this was an area he had always felt less than adequate in, he very carefully said, "I did once."

Mattie fixed him with a gaze that was edged with sarcasm. "When?"

"When I met you." She burst into laughter and tears simultaneously, leaning into his arms when he opened them to her. "Matt, I hate to see you give up on this." He rubbed his hand over her shoulders as he consoled her. "I know things have been shitty lately," he counseled. "I just don't think you're thinking about this clearly."

"But it's so hard!" she moaned. "What if I can't do it?"

"You *can* do it." He thought about it for a little while. "Maybe this isn't the right place for you to be, that's all. We should go to LA." Before she could protest he added, "A friend of mine from university lives down there now. I could try to swing a job with him. I know you probably wouldn't be able to work there, but we can live on one income for a while. It won't kill us. We'll stay until you sign a recording contract."

This time she was able to protest. "I can't ask you to pick up and move just because of me."

"Why not?"

"Because your whole family is here."

"So what?" She gave him the same sarcastic look again, and he laughed. "That's what telephones and airplanes are for, Matt. We'll move anywhere that you want to go."

Her eyes shimmered with tears again. "Really?"

His smile widened, and his affection for her deepened when he told her, "Absolutely."

> We're still talking about moving to California. After a lot of discussion, Mark made me realize that I had given up on my music career because I thought I had to, and that I would have been absolutely miserable if I'd actually walked away from it.
>
> Have I mentioned how much I love that man?
>
> Mark's friend says that he has a job whenever he wants it. We're just trying to decide whether or not he'll keep his partnership shares with the company. Having that money back would certainly make the move a lot easier.

Chapter 38

Helen was in the middle of preparing dinner for the kids when a wave of nausea overtook her, sending her for the bathroom at a run. She'd barely managed to make it to the toilet bowl before she threw up, leaving an open door in her wake. Paul had followed her when he saw her run out, cautiously sticking his head around the side of the door to see what was happening. He could see his mother heaving, and it scared him. "Mom?"

She didn't actually hear him until her system had settled down again, then was horrified to see his 10-year-old face watching her with such adult concern. "I'm okay, Honey," she told him amidst coughs. "Nothing to worry about."

"You sure?" he asked, handing her a towel when she silently asked for it.

"I'm fine, Paulie," she reassured him, pulling him in for a hug when he came near her. "It's just the baby – when a lady is having a baby, she gets sick for the first little while." He fixed her with a funny look. "I'm okay," she reassured again. "Really." After hugging him one more time she suggested, "Why don't you go grab your homework so I can take a look at it."

He hesitantly did as he was told, leaving her alone to clean up before heading back to the kitchen. She rinsed her mouth with a handful of water, catching a glimpse of herself in the mirror. Her skin was pale, especially in comparison to the fading bruise on her cheek. She sighed. It seemed that the only time Kevin spent at home now was long enough to knock her around or knock her up. When she was younger, she'd always thought that she wanted a big family. But with

Number Five now on the way, she realized that she had also envisioned that family living in a large house, with a father who actually helped out and spent time with them.

A scream and crying from her youngest daughter ripped her from her reflection and back into the dining area. Susanne was howling in pain, her toddler arms not able to fend off the blows that her older sister was inflicting on her. "Katrina!" she shouted, grabbing the offender by the arm and spanking her as she hauled her off into the living room.

"Mommy no!" Katrina cried, running off to the kids' room as soon as she could wrestle herself free.

Helen stopped in mid-stroke, horrified at her own reaction. She never laid a hand on the kids, and she collapsed onto her knees when she realized what had just happened. Between her hitting Katrina and Katrina hitting her little sister, it was thoroughly disturbing. Her hands shook and her heart pounded while her mind raced. "Oh my god," she moaned as she burst into tears. "Oh my god!"

Later on that night, after the kids were all in bed, Helen still found herself haunted by what had happened. The kids had fought before, but she had never seen one of them so blatantly attacking another. Or at least any previous instances could be explained away or simply ignored.

She felt horrible inside. *I've allowed this to happen,* she thought to herself as she chewed on her nails. As her mind processed what had happened, she realized that it indeed was not the first time that Katrina had mimicked her father's violent behavior. It was just the first time that Helen allowed herself to draw a link between the two.

She hadn't thought seriously about leaving in quite some time, though the idea did cross her mind every time she socked a little bit of money away into her secret account. Thankfully Kevin wasn't too diligent when it came to where she spent the money he gave her. But she was thinking hard now. She wondered what would happen if they stayed; how the kids would turn out if they continued to be exposed to the violence between their parents.

The pictures on the wall caught her attention as they frequently did. The wedding photos that Kevin had insisted she keep out were now supplemented by family photos, and as she gazed at the last family portrait she started to cry. They looked happy – but in a way that usually ended up on true crime shows with voiceovers of neighbors saying, *"They seemed like such a normal family…"*

The switch finally flipped. Kevin was off for the weekend fishing with his buddies, and he had left the car behind because someone else drove. She wasn't going to get a better opportunity than this.

It only took a couple of hours to pack enough things into the car for the kids, though she was careful not to disturb them until the last minute. She was on her way to get them when she stopped in the living room, to see if there was anything she wanted to take. Her eyes scanned over everything, eventually landing on the entertainment center again. All of the pictures contained Kevin, which she really didn't want right now. *Or at all,* she thought. But there was one that he wasn't in, and she walked over to examine it.

It was a photo of her, Graham and Mattie, taken at the twenty-fifth birthday party that Mattie had thrown for her. The only reason she had kept it out was because Kevin had once commented on how good a picture it was of her. Helen had forgotten how generous Mattie had always tried to be with her friends, making sure that their achievements were celebrated or that they had a shoulder to cry on. It also caused her to have a blind spot, especially when it came to Graham. Helen suddenly felt another pang of loneliness hit her. When she had received Mattie's harsh letter she had gotten angry, so angry at the woman who was her best friend. And the anger had made it so much easier to hate her. But try as she might, Helen could never forget her.

She took the frame and stuffed it into the top of her duffel bag before putting the kids into the car and heading for Edmonton.

Chapter 39

It turns out that moving to Los Angeles was just the help that my career needed. I can't explain it, but everything seemed to catch fire as soon as we crossed the border. I secured a recording contract, and the record company released a test single to see how it would do on radio. It did great, so I will shortly be embarking on a small tour of the western continent. It's a series of small, intimate venues – five hundred or less – just me and my piano. Well, as intimate as five hundred people can get.

The powers that be didn't want to include Edmonton, but I made them. Besides, why should I pay to go home and visit everyone when it can be taken care of by someone else?

Mattie could not have been more enthralled with the results of the tour, and though she didn't fill every venue, the crowds that turned up did so in encouraging numbers. Performing was something that she had always relished, but it was particularly special when she felt a strong connection with the audience. She could tell in the first few seconds of walking onstage whether or not she would have the room in the palm of her hand. Fortunately, she usually did.

Mark took time off from work in order to accompany her on the trip, though in the course of six weeks he did have to return to Los Angeles twice to secure accounts that had been put in jeopardy by clients who got jittery in his absence. He usually watched from a secluded place in each venue where she wouldn't be able to see him; they had quickly learned that his presence could be distracting to her while on stage, so they came to an arrangement where he would be buried in the crowd or in a private box. She always knew he was there, but *out of sight, out of mind* seemed to apply.

The last of the concerts took place in Edmonton, which was designed in order for her to be able to spend the Christmas holidays with her family and oldest friends. And being a hometown girl, she had managed to pack the small theater. It made for a warm atmosphere, mostly because of the friends that had come to see her before the show. From her solitary place on stage she could see them, which gave her the opportunity to talk to some of them during the show.

She settled into a powerful ballad about halfway through, not her own song, but one that had struck a chord with her years before. As she performed, she stared out into the eyes of the audience before her, a thought of *I wonder what they're thinking?* flickering through her mind.

Scanning the faces as she continued to sing, her smile widened when she saw Zack seated on the stage right side of the front row. She hadn't really expected him to come, especially in light of how they had parted company. The memory of the last time they saw each other flooded back to her. The irony of it was that it was the same place that they had originally met – the hallway between their apartments.

She was piling boxes beside the elevator door when he came out and, true to form, Max raced through his door before Zack could catch him. With a grumble he hunted the cat down, grinning a little when he saw a tail poking out

*from behind his new amp. "C'mere you," he grunted,
reaching down and picking Max up.*

*When he returned to the hall, his neighbor was nowhere
to be found. So Max received more than adequate attention
while they waited. Mattie appeared a few seconds later,
barely able to see over the box she was carrying. She
stopped short when she saw them, and then she sighed,
"Max..."*

*"He always did like my place best," he commented
quietly, refusing to relinquish his hold on the cat.*

*It took a long time for her to find her voice, but she
eventually agreed, "Yeah, I guess he has." They locked eyes
for a moment, then she turned away to carry the box to the
elevator. On her pass back she took Max into her arms and
scolded, "You'd better not act like this in Vancouver."*

*"Vancouver?" His words failed to stop her momentum,
so he followed her back into her place. She was just setting
the cat down in the middle of the living room when he found
her. "Why didn't you tell me you're leaving?"*

*She shot him a pointed look. "You'd better get out of
here before your wife catches you."*

*Zack grimaced – he really had not planned on getting
into this again. "Come on, Matt. Cut me a little slack, will
you?"*

*Now she turned to face him front on, arms defiantly
folded across her chest. "Why should I?"*

"What?"

*"You heard me." She turned back to stare out the
curtainless window.*

He demanded, "Why are you punishing me?"

*Mattie whirled back on him. "Because you screwed me
over for Rhonda. Because your sex life obviously means
more to you than our friendship. You won't even talk to me
because she's forbidden you to. If you don't have the balls to
stand up for yourself, then I can't be bothered to worry
about you." With breath heaving in her chest, she turned*

back to the landscape outside. "Just don't expect me to come running when your marriage falls apart."

He stared at her, stunned, for a long while. It wasn't as if he hadn't seen it coming, he just never expected to ever see it. She waited with the patience of a saint, refusing to say another word to him. If she did, she might lose it altogether. His head dropped when he finally admitted defeat, and he silently left.

Mattie suddenly realized that she had been lost in thought. Looking down at the keys, she was surprised to see her fingers still moving coherently, along with a strong voice that had continued to sing the correct words. Cursing herself for her lapse, she threw herself into the rest of the song. She took a break for water when it was done, taking the opportunity to examine the reaction. She seemed to have gotten through the lapse without anybody noticing. A quick look at Zack's beaming expression was enough to convince her of that.

In the wings, Mark watched her with some worry. She happened to glance in his direction, catching his eye and giving him a nod that confirmed that she was okay, and that she would explain later. Her lips curled into a smile when he returned the nod, and then stepped back to disappear out of her sight again.

Chapter 40

The basement in Les and Jennifer's house was packed full a few days later, assembled for one of their famous movie parties. A large, highly-charged variety of people made several trips up and down the stairs that ran from the basement, past the back door and up into the kitchen. Jennifer and Mattie were busy carrying trays of hot food down so that everything would be laid out before the movie started, adept navigation keeping the men from getting their hands on the wings until they could set them down on the coffee table.

The doorbell rang. "I wonder who that is," Jennifer said. A quick glance around her showed that everyone that had been invited was there already. "I'll be right back," she told her husband as she headed for the stairs.

Mattie was immediately behind her, saying, "We forgot a bowl for bones." She veered off into the kitchen while her friend headed for the front door. Almost as new in this house as the owners were, she had to search through a couple of cupboards in order to find what she was looking for. The conversation at the door played absently in her mind, but only for just a few seconds. She noticed a squeal of delight from Jennifer, which was followed by a voice that she had not heard in many, many years.

"Oh my god!" Jennifer gasped as she let go of the visitor at the door. "What are you doing here?"

Helen shrugged, a sheepish grin crossing her lips. "I was just in the neighborhood," she joked. Her arm reached behind her, a slight twist in her body as she indicated the large number of cars parked out at the curb. "Am I interrupting?"

"Absolutely not," the other told her. "Can you stay?" After a moment's hesitation Helen agreed, handing her ratty, down-filled jacket to the hostess as soon as she slipped it off. The two of them started a fast and furious conversation as Jennifer led the way through the house, not noticing anything out of the ordinary when Mattie was not in the kitchen. The movie's start was delayed for at least ten minutes when everyone was involved in hugs and introductions, and more questions than Helen cared to answer.

Jennifer headed back upstairs in order to retrieve the drink that Helen had requested. Mark had noticed that his wife had not come back downstairs with the two of them, and he sensed that something was amiss. He set his can of beer down on the table and went up into the kitchen. "Hey Jen," he greeted when he saw her pulling a bottle of cola out of the fridge.

"Hey Gorgeous," she replied with a smile.

He leaned the small of his back against the edge of the counter. "You haven't seen my wife, have you?"

Jennifer's hand was reaching into the cupboard to get a glass, the motion stopping when she realized what was happening. "Now that you mention it," she told him, "I haven't seen her since Helen showed up."

"Helen?" He glanced back down the basement stairs like he would be able to see her, then looked back at the party's hostess again. "*The* Helen?"

She nodded, the glass hitting the counter with a sharp bang. "That's her."

Mattie's husband looked back down the stairs again, a crease forming in his brow when everything fell into place. He knew exactly where his wife had gone. She may have quit smoking, but she still ran outside when faced with great stress. Jennifer was slowly unscrewing the cap on the bottle when she saw him snatch his jacket off the hook and head out the back door.

She was out freezing in the shelter of the unheated garage as he predicted, pacing a narrow path from one end of the building to the other. She stopped briefly between the cars when she saw him enter, then continued on. Mark closed the door behind him and shoved his exposed hand back into his pocket immediately afterward. "You okay?" he asked.

"Oh yeah, sure," she told him as she continued to travel, her voice dripping. "Everything's fine. Everything's just fucking wonderful!" For a moment she faced him and sharply added, "And how are things with you?"

"Mattie..."

"Don't tell me that I'm overreacting!" his wife spat at him. She turned her back on him, her fingers nervously pulling at each other.

"Come on." He walked toward her, and when she didn't try to sidestep him, he gently stilled her hands. "You can't avoid her, Matt." Then he pulled her close, his hands resting on her shoulders as he looked at her. "I'm sure that she didn't expect to find you here either."

"How could she?" Mattie sniffled loudly, trying valiantly not to start crying. "How can she just show up here?"

"I don't know."

"I don't want to talk to her."

Through the window of the small garage door, Mark could see the woman in question approaching through the cold. "I don't think you have a choice." He leaned down and kissed her forehead, then left her and said hello to Helen in passing at the door.

Mattie's gaze followed him until the door was opened, and she could see who was on the other side. Quickly turning around, she kept her back to the woman who she now considered a stranger. Helen came inside, leaving the door open behind her because it simply did not occur to her to close it. "Hello Mattie," she said tentatively, keeping her distance. When the other did not answer she had to think. "I didn't expect to see you here."

"Well you shouldn't expect a lot," Mattie advised. "It just leads to disappointment."

Helen caught herself nodding and forced her head to remain still. Grasping at straws forced her to say, "You look great."

There was a long pause. "Thanks," the other said tersely, starting to pace again. "You've put on weight."

Helen stared at her, unable to believe that she was receiving this kind of treatment from her. Then again, she really didn't expect any other kind of reaction from Mattie either. "I...uh..." She stopped, trying to get a handle on her stammering. A lighthearted attempt was made when she said, "So...what's new?"

Mattie took the time to draw in a deep breath before turning around to face Helen. "Oh nothing much," she told her flippantly. "I'm just back in town visiting family and friends. Which reminds me...you haven't seen one of them have you? About five six, a hundred and nine pounds, blonde hair and no spine?"

"Look, I came to make peace," Helen countered as she stuffed her hands into her pockets.

"So what?"

Helen stared at her, dumbfounded. "This was a bad idea," she murmured before turning and heading for the door.

"Is that it?" Mattie questioned from her place in front of the cars. Helen stopped, but did not turn around. "You came all the way out here, and you're going to give up that easy?" She regarded the other woman, looking her up and down. "Oh yeah, I forgot. You turn tail and run at the first sign of disagreement."

Now Helen turned to face her. "What is that supposed to mean?"

"Don't tell me you've forgotten." Mattie only gave her a split second to fill in a response before giving it to her. "Your fiancé attacks me on the floor of your bedroom, but you marry him anyway. You get pregnant, and despite my warnings you let him cut you off from your family and move you to his little hometown where he could have complete control of you."

Helen reeled back a bit, Mattie's words hitting too close to home. "Is that what you think?" she challenged.

"Pretty much." Mattie started to fiddle with the items on Les's tool bench, unable to look Helen in the eye. "You were supposed to be my friend. You were supposed to meet Jen and me when you were in town, so that we could see *our friend*." The wrench dropped back down onto the bench with a loud bang. "But you didn't have the balls to at least tell us you weren't coming."

"Now wait just a goddamn minute." Helen stalked over and pointed a badly chipped fingernail into the other's face. "Ending our relationship wasn't my idea. I wasn't the one with the poison pen!"

Mattie knocked the finger out of her face and stalked past her and into the confined space between the cars. "You didn't leave me any choice. Kevin meant more to you than I did – you made that perfectly clear. But what you couldn't see was that he destroyed the person I knew, every time he was around. When I visited you in Valleyview, he lurked around just to make sure that I wasn't going to be a bad influence and, God forbid, force you to think for yourself again!"

"How dare you!" Helen shouted back at her, her hands clenching at her sides. "How dare you stand there and tell me fairy tales about what you think my life should be! You don't know the first thing about Kevin–"

"You're right," Mattie cut her off, "I don't. But I know you. You were so desperate to have a baby that you hooked up with the first thing that stuck around long enough to conceive one!" Helen tried to argue against the point, but Mattie was on a tirade, and all the pent-up emotion and sorrow over their ruined relationship rocketed to the surface. After more than a decade, everything that Mattie had ever thought about saying was so ingrained in her mind that she didn't have to think about it. "Do you know what it feels like to have your best friend ask you to be there when her child is born? And do you know what it's like when your friend then says that she's suddenly giving up everything that she's known and moving away to join her husband, who has never lifted a finger to try and keep his promise to her?" Tears started to fill Mattie's eyes. "Do you know how much you hurt me? How robbed I felt because I wasn't going to be there with you? You ripped my heart out!" The tears that she had attempted to control now streamed down her cheeks when she confessed, "I have never felt as worthless and alone as I did when you dropped me for him."

Helen stopped to consider everything that had just been hurled at her. "What else was I supposed to do?" she spat back, taking a couple of challenging steps toward Mattie, who had partly turned away from her. "I was about to have a baby. I couldn't do that by myself!"

"You weren't going to be by yourself!"

"You were hardly a replacement for a husband!" Mattie opened her mouth, but Helen shot her a look of contempt sharp enough to silence her. "You can't know what it's like to be part of a marriage. Marriage is compromise."

"It's a partnership," Mattie countered as she spun around. "And I *do* know what it's like." She paused, seeing the look of disbelief she was receiving. "I am married," she flatly stated. "If you would have bothered to call in the past ten years you would know that."

Helen was shocked. Since it had been so long since they had seen each other, she still thought of Mattie as the miserable single hooked onto an unavailable man. "You're what?"

Mattie ripped off a leather glove to reveal the stones she wore. "Married. M-A-R-R-I-E-D!" She paused with melodramatic flair, sarcastically adding, "I'm sure you recognize the term."

The other folded her arms over her chest again, cold beginning to creep inside her coat. "I never asked for your approval. Only for you to support my choices. But you couldn't even do that!"

"What was I supposed to say? I love you, but your husband is an idiot? That he scared the shit out of me, and that I was afraid he would do worse to you? I couldn't live with the worry of what he might do to you every day!"

"That's it!" Helen roared. "I am not going to stand here and apologize to you for the decisions I've made in my life. It's none of your goddamn business anyway!" A sharp turn led her directly to the door that started the path back through the snow to the house.

"Fine!" Mattie took a threatening step toward her. "Walk away, just like you did before. Don't write, don't phone. Don't bother to worry about me. I've managed to get on without you before. I'm sure it won't be hard for me to do again!" To punctuate the finality, she again turned her back on the other.

Helen stared at her for a few moments, her hand resting on the knob of the open garage door. Her ears rang with Mattie's accusations, and they did not sit easily on her conscience. "Is that what you think?" she asked again.

This time Mattie did not turn back. Her voice was strained, and she was clearly weary of this argument. Though she was unwilling to carry on, she couldn't help but ask, "Is *what* what I think?"

Helen took a cautious step further inside, but kept her hand on the knob as a type of safety line. "Do you think I never thought of you?" she questioned. "I was always surrounded by the pictures from my wedding. And every day when I looked at them, I saw you. I saw the woman that I loved more than my own sister." She stopped to collect her thoughts again, and took another deep breath of frigid winter air. "But I couldn't be so selfish as to put myself over the interests of my kids. So I sat there, day after day, looking at all those pictures. And I thought about the way that you and I had talked about the future. And how different it was supposed to be." She paused, waiting for some kind of answer. When she didn't hear one, she finally told her, "Mattie, I left him."

There was the key, the words that were enough to tear Mattie's attention from the spot her eyes had bored into the wall in front of her. She squinted, accentuating the lines around her eyes and mouth as she stared at Helen. With a plume of frost she breathed, "You what?"

Helen nodded. "The kids and I have been living with a friend here in the city. Kevin hasn't seen us for nearly four months now." Her voice started to quiver, and it was quite apparent to Mattie that she was seething with anger at both of them. She had been all along. "He hasn't even tried to see his own kids."

Suddenly awkward, Mattie mumbled, "I'm sorry."

"Don't be." Helen sat down on the front end of Les's car, her sign of utter defeat. She had a lost look in her expression, and for the first time Mattie could see the mental exhaustion that the woman had been quietly suffering with. "You were right about him." She sighed. "He became everything you said he would."

The news sent a pang through Mattie's chest. She had believed in her heart of hearts that Kevin was going to become abusive – but hearing it confirmed was enough to make her cry. She slowly sat down beside Helen, saying nothing. After a while she suddenly questioned, "How many kids?"

Helen sniffled a bit. "Five."

They lapsed into a long stretch of silence again, each reliving their time apart and the missed friendship that they could have had. Mattie murmured, "Will you look at us." Helen nodded her agreement, and they lapsed into another pause. Mattie eventually asked her, "Is it too late to try this again?"

Helen shrugged. "It'll take time."

They looked at each other, and the tension eased only slightly when they broke into cautious smiles. The cold quickly drove them back into the house, where Mattie declined to answer any questions until she could do so in private, and she took shelter in her husband's arms when they finally started the movies.

Chapter 41

Mattie set a bundle of beat-up hardcover notebooks down between them. "What's this?" her friend questioned as she picked them up, turning them over and over in her hands to examine them.

"Letters." Mattie chewed on a piece of ice, and swallowed it before she explained, "I never stopped writing to you all these years."

Helen pulled one of the books out from between the elastic bands as Mattie took another mouthful of ice. She flipped through some of them and stopped about halfway through, then started reading the precisely sculpted blue letters. It was chronicling the end of the relationship with Graham, and Helen had no problem deciphering the anguish in Mattie's words. She looked up at her friend, whose eyes had momentarily slid closed. "Why didn't you ever send them?"

"You never would have read them," she replied softly. "Especially after what I said."

Helen nodded, "Maybe," and returned to her reading. It covered most of the relationships with Zack and Mark, and Helen was a little shocked by the candid nature of the entries. It finally occurred to her that these were more than just letters to an absent friend – it was a diary. Helen looked up at her again. "Are you sure you want me to read these?" Her friend didn't answer, but her eyes were now tightly squeezed shut. "Matt?"

Mattie was forced to let go of her held breath, hissing, "This is a big one."

Helen was instantly on her feet, laying the book pages-down onto the mattress. Her hands rubbed some of the ache from Mattie's back as she leaned forward into the contraction, and Helen reminded herself to observe what was happening. And when it was done, she took her place back at her friend's side and continued to watch.

Mattie laid her head back into the pillow, the tension slowly draining from her face while she concentrated on breathing. After a while she said, "I never would have given them to you if I didn't want you to read them." When her eyes opened again, she looked at the clock on the other side of the room. "When did Mark say he was going to get here?"

"Not for a couple of hours yet. The plane didn't leave Tampa until three." She saw the hurt look in Mattie's eyes and assured her, "Don't worry, he'll be here."

Mattie nodded, a small smile creeping into her expression. She reached her hand out, and felt Helen's warmth quickly surround it. "Well…"

"Well." Helen gave her friend's hand a slight squeeze. Her own grin broadened when she commented, "Looks like we finally got here, huh?"

"Yeah," Mattie agreed. "But I still would have preferred it the other way around."

"Forget it. I've already done this bit."

The pair settled back into the easy, lighthearted banter that had taken them years to perfect. They were well on the way to repairing their friendship, and it contented Mattie to a level that she hadn't been at in more than a decade. She had reunited with her soul mate.